Kaine's Sanction

Shattered Empire, Volume 1

D.M. Pruden

Published by Fuzzy Slipper Publishing, 2019.

FREE EBOOK OFFER!

As a way of saying thank you for purchasing this novel, I want to offer you a free ebook.

To claim your free story please join my reader list by going to
https://www.prudenauthor.com/Kaine1-free-offer

Invaded

BLOOD RAN FROM THE open gash on the admiral's scalp.

The pungent scent of smoke and dust gave her an idea of the damage they'd suffered.

"Give me the defence status report."

"The surface is under heavy bombardment," said the second officer. "The orbital hub is destroyed."

"How many ships survived?"

"Six, Admiral; four of them are civilian vessels. One transport and three freighters."

"Where did they come from?" she said to her XO, Commander Gill.

The right side of his face was a bloody, burned mess, but he remained at his station, despite the obvious pain.

Even though the military command centre was buried beneath kilometres of bedrock, they had been hit hard. Half of her staff were dead or critically injured. She could only imagine the extent of the devastation to Dulcinea's settlements on the ground.

"They are employing some kind of stealth technology, Admiral," said Gill. "We can't see them to shoot back, and I have never seen anything like the weapons they are using."

"Nor I, and I spent six years at the Tactical Research Centre on Earth."

"Where would one of the factions get tech like this?"

"They want to separate from the Confederation, not start a war," she said. "None of the dissenting colonies have shown military aggression before."

"Well, then who could they be?"

Another violent earthquake shook the reinforced foundations.

"That was a big one," said the admiral. "What the hell could they be using to bombard the planet?"

1

"Sir," said the second officer. "The *Revenge* and *Victory* are destroyed."

"That's the last of our orbital defences," said Gill, "and they are picking off our surface installations from orbit."

"Did you reach the governor yet?"

"No, ma'am. The Parliamentary Palace is gone. We must assume every cabinet minister is dead."

"That just leaves me," she said. "Send out a general broadcast. Announce our surrender."

"The attackers don't respond to any of our hails."

"What other choice is there?"

Another blast knocked everyone from their feet. A trickle of dust fell on the admiral's face as she lay on the floor, stunned.

The reinforced ceiling cracked under the strain of kilometres of overburden.

Everything crashed down on her.

Forty Years Later

"WAKE UP, ASSHOLE! YOU'LL be late for inspection."

Hayden Kaine hated alarms. Avoidance of discipline and schedules was one reason he had deactivated his LINK's chronometric functions. Of course, that never prevented his roommate from serving that role on his own initiative. If not for Kyle's adherence to the rules on his behalf, he didn't believe he would have survived academy life. As things were, the two of them enjoyed a codependent relationship that served them both, though he often felt he got the better end of the deal.

"I'm awake. Stop shouting." He dragged the sheets over his head.

"You need to be up, Officer Cadet Kaine." Kyle emphasized his point by yanking the covers from his friend.

Hayden pulled the pillow over his head and curled into a fetal position. "Just three more days, Mom?"

Deciding he could no longer put it off, he sat on the edge of the bed and blinked at the sunshine streaming through the opened blinds.

"Whose bright idea was it to get an apartment facing east?"

"It faces west, thanks to your influential daddy. Of course, you might remember that if you spent any significant time here," called Kyle from the kitchen.

Hayden cradled his head in his hands and moaned. "Are you still dating that medical student? Do you think she can get me some really powerful painkillers, or just something to kill me?"

"Her name is Andrea, and she's my fiancée, if it makes any difference. These should help."

He looked up to Kyle, holding a steaming cup of coffee in one hand and a pair of white medicine tablets in the other.

After tossing the pills to the back of his throat, he gulped down half the beverage, oblivious to its temperature.

"What the hell happened to you last night? You usually show some modicum of self-control the night before a parade inspection."

Hayden's shoulders slumped, and he cradled the cup in both hands while he stared at the late afternoon sun.

"Katie and I broke up."

Kyle regarded his roommate, a deep frown creasing his brow. "You asshole! She was the best thing to ever happen to you. Who did the breaking up?"

"Technically, it was her."

"And, 'technically,' what was her reason this time?"

He winced in recollection. "She walked in on me in bed with Sharon."

Hayden didn't see the fist that caught him in the side of his jaw and sent him to the floor and the remains of his coffee splattering the wall.

"You...oh! There are no words to describe you. What the hell would tempt you to cheat on Katie?"

"I don't have a good reason, okay? She blew our date off because of some big assignment from her granddad, and, well, we argued, and I went drinking and...it just happened."

"Holy Mary, Mother of God! You are such a dog! Just a week before graduation, and you pull a stunt like that. It probably explains the priority message from the Old Man flashing for you on the board."

"What are you talking about?" Hayden sat up, rubbing his chin. When Kyle didn't bother to answer, he stood and made his way to the comm panel. On the way, he activated and reviewed the messages cued on his LINK but saw nothing from Admiral Thomas. The Old Man, as he often did when he was about to release a disciplinary shitstorm on someone, had gone old-school and posted on the public board. Nobody other than the recipient could access the contents, but the meaning of it being there was understood by every cadet in the academy.

Aware of Kyle's scrutiny, he accessed and read the communiqué. After a few moments, Kyle said, "Well? What does it say?"

"He's summoned me to his office for a special assignment." He stared at the screen, trying to decipher the hidden meaning behind the short missive.

"What the hell, man? He must really be pissed with you. What do you think it is?"

"Well, he can't flunk me. Despite my best efforts, I did manage to meet the grad requirements."

"Holy shit, man. Where do you think he'll send you? I heard that he once assigned a graduate to spend his first five years in sewage maintenance..."

"I don't think that's what this is about."

"Huh? How can you be so sure? He's never liked the idea of you dating his precious little genius granddaughter. Now that you spectacularly screwed that relationship up..."

"Katie isn't like that. She never told the Old Man about our...issues. She wouldn't do it now."

"A woman scorned and all..."

Hayden glared at him.

"Okay, Kaine. What do you think it is?"

"It might be a consular posting."

"What? Are you nuts?"

"No, I don't think so. Dad's pressed hard for me at the Admiralty. I did specialize in diplomatic relations."

He deleted the message and moved to the closet to select his uniform.

"When is the meeting?"

"Geneva, later today."

"There is an inspection parade this evening. What will I tell Warrant Officer Singh?"

Hayden shrugged. "Admiral's orders, I suppose. It was on the public board."

Kyle shook his head. "If you get shipped off to some wreck to run radiation leak maintenance, I want you to pay what you owe me before you go."

"That is not going to happen. Besides, if it is, I'm sure I'll be given time to pack." He smiled at his long-time friend, who rolled his eyes and retreated to his own bedroom.

It had to be a diplomatic posting. What other reason for a personal meeting? Any other assignment would come through the routine, post-graduation assignations that every cadet received. It wouldn't be for any kind of retribution over his indiscretion. Whatever happened between he and Katie remained strictly beyond the Old Man's ability to redress without legal implications for the admiral.

Dad came through. Hayden pumped his fist in private celebration. He and his father always agreed that a military commission would be valuable on the resume, but only as a stepping-stone to the diplomatic corps. From there, after a few years' experience in various postings of increasing importance, he would run for election to the governing council, as planned.

This meeting had to be for a high-profile commission, accelerated by the brewing dispute between colonial factions. He would probably be assigned to a Peace Keeper ship and assist in calming things down. A perfect first assignment. His father would be pleased.

The thought of being sent so far away gave Hayden pause. He should call Katie and try to pour oil on the waters before he was shipped off. There was no long-term plan for their relationship; they both understood their careers would carry them in different directions, but he didn't want them to part after an unresolved transgression.

She had a generous and forgiving spirit. He realized it was the primary reason she had put up with his bullshit for so long, but he worried he'd gone too far this time. He resolved to call on her and beg for forgiveness. They probably wouldn't make up, but it could be his only chance to say goodbye.

But first, he had a more pressing matter to attend to before his departure for Geneva.

Pausing, he accessed his LINK to transfer the funds he owed to Kyle's account.

Iris

IRIS MONTAGUE-BREYSON was the most brilliant person Hayden knew.

After an accomplished career as the preeminent researcher in multidimensional physics, she "retired" to be a full-time instructor at the academy. She was known as an uncompromising taskmaster who brooked nothing short of perfection from her students. As a result, over two-thirds of the cadets who took her course failed on their first attempt.

Most people believed Katie's help allowed Hayden to pass Iris's class on his first try. Nothing could be further from the truth.

Though she was one of his toughest teachers, nearly failing him on more assignments than he cared to recall, she held a special place in his heart.

When his mother, Amelia, died, it was her best friend, Iris, who stepped up to help bring up six-year-old Hayden. Walden Kaine's career and ambition kept him far too preoccupied to sacrifice the time necessary to raise his traumatized son.

With no children or family of her own, she took on the role with the same brilliant dedication to perfection she devoted to her professional life. Somehow, the woman whose life was just as demanding as his father's had created the time to become his surrogate mother.

Through his father's influence, he gained admission to the elite Confederation Military Academy. But it was his desire to make Iris proud that motivated him to succeed in his studies.

Hayden passed the course because he did not want to disappoint his "Auntie I."

Period.

It was the most challenging time of his education and taught him the necessary discipline to apply himself — when he chose to do so, which was less often than she liked.

The palliative care unit was a brightly lit, sunny place. In many ways, it was like Iris herself.

Hayden greeted the nurses with a familiar nod as he walked past the charge desk.

"How is she today, Penny?"

"She took a turn last night," said the pretty young nurse. "And before you get upset, she ordered me not to contact you unless something 'definitively imminent' developed. Her words."

He shook his head. "Typical. Is she awake?"

"She's in the sunroom."

Hayden plucked a daisy from the bouquet he'd brought and gave it to her on his way to locate Iris.

He found her in an armchair with her back to the door. A wool blanket covered her up to her neck, despite the warm sunshine that streamed into the room.

She heard him before he could speak and turned, smiling.

It had been too many weeks since his last visit. She was a gaunt shadow of the robust, energetic Auntie I of his childhood.

He did his best to bury his feelings and returned her smile. He pulled up a chair and presented the flowers to her.

"Oh, for me? And daisies, too. Thank you, dear."

She accepted them with shaking hands and set them down on the side table.

"Let me look at you," she said as she grasped his hands. Her grip was far stronger than he expected. "You aren't eating properly. Perhaps partying a little too much, eh?" She winked.

He blushed. "Possibly."

"How is that lovely girlfriend of yours?"

He examined the pattern of the carpet and after an uncomfortable pause told her everything. He kept no secrets from her.

She shook her head. "Oh, I'm so sorry this happened."

That was all.

No admonition; no disappointment in her voice or judgement in her tone. Just acceptance.

"Admiral Thomas summoned me to his office. For an assignment."

She nodded. "Feeling a little nervous, are you?"

"Yes. I'm not sure what to expect after..."

"He has no legal right to use that situation to justify personal revenge. If he does, he will hear from me. I still maintain a few connections over his head at that place."

Hayden smiled. "Thanks, but I don't think it will come to that. At least I hope not. But I am concerned about leaving you behind if he sends me off somewhere."

"Don't worry about me." She patted his hand.

"But, I..."

"Honey, it is time you come to terms with the fact that I'm not long for this life. I accept that, and you must as well. I tried to teach you all you need, given your father's expectations of you."

He frowned and shook his head. "Dad doesn't realize—"

"No, Hayden. *You* don't realize. He sacrificed everything for you. You don't think so, but it is true. He may not be the father of the year, but he cares for you. He cared enough to ask me to raise you, rather than cede your upbringing to boarding schools. Don't judge him too harshly."

She released his hand and picked up a folio from the side table. "This is important. Read it before you leave here."

"Now?"

"Yes, now. We don't need to talk to enjoy each other's company. I want to discuss something about that with you when you're finished. Take your time. I'm not going anywhere."

She closed her eyes and leaned back in the armchair.

Hayden guiltily checked his chronometer. He needed to catch Katie before his departure to Geneva, but...

He opened the folio. It contained a scientific brief from a research section he was not familiar with.

"Am I cleared to read this?"

"Oh, tosh-tosh. You won't tell anyone, and nobody would believe you if you did."

Hayden settled into the chair and began reading. The report was from some archaeological researcher stuck out in the boonies. He claimed that he had uncovered an extinct alien culture on one of the outermost colony planets. The location was blacked out, as were a lot of the details, but what he could read seemed more like a science fiction novel than a serious report.

"Is this real? Who is this crackpot?"

"You'll note his name is redacted. I'm not privy to who he is, but I have my suspicions. And to answer your question, yes, it is."

"But this is outlandish. A dead race of sentient aliens? We've been stepping out into the galaxy for the last three centuries. No life form more advanced than bacteria has ever been encountered."

"You recall the Drake hypothesis? Who is to say that other cultures did not exist in the past? The universe is far older than our solar system."

"Why are you showing this to me?"

"If Thomas is sending you where I think he might, it will be useful for you to go with an open mind."

"I realize that, but this?"

Iris began to chuckle, which soon devolved into a coughing fit. She seemed not to be able to catch her breath.

Hayden ran out to the front desk and found Penny.

Twenty minutes later, she was in her bed, hooked up to oxygen and intravenous drips. She looked up at him with rheumy eyes and tried to speak.

"Don't talk," he said as he hovered over her.

She ignored him and spoke anyway, her voice muffled by the mask. "You will be late for your appointments. Go and see your girl. Ask for forgiveness, even if neither of you believe you deserve it. And promise me you will see your father before you are sent off-world."

"I'll come back to say goodbye, if that happens." His eyes were moist.

She shook her head. "This is our farewell, my boy." Her shaking hands gently caressed his face. "I could never have loved you as much as your mother did, but I gave you my whole heart. Forgive me for being too hard on you."

Tears flowed down his cheeks. "You weren't..."

"Oh, tosh-tosh. Give me a kiss and be on your way."

Hayden leaned over and kissed her on the forehead. "Goodbye, Auntie. I love you."

Iris did not respond, having lapsed into sleep.

Penny spoke softly. "All we can do at this point is manage her pain."

"You'll inform me of any changes in her condition?"

She nodded.

Depending on what the admiral had planned for him, he was concerned he might never see Auntie I again.

HAYDEN TURNED THE COLD cup of coffee in his hands as he watched the faces of the passersby. They were all focused on some destination, and few would normally give someone loitering on a bench more than a cursory glance. This time, he attracted far more attention than he found comfortable.

It was the dress uniform, of course.

Most of the crowd in lab coats, rushing for their lunch break, regarded him like he was some interloper.

Though the research campus was part of the academy, few uniforms ever ventured here. The researchers did not wish to acknowledge they were still a branch of the military, preferring to believe they worked for interests more altruistic than those of the empire.

His presence offended them, but Katie's refusal to return his pings had left him with little choice.

Hanging around outside her place of work was, perhaps, not the best plan, but it was all he had time for. His shuttle was due to depart in a couple of hours.

She must be really pissed this time, he thought.

He spotted her seconds before she saw him. Her shoulders slumped in resignation, and she said something to her two companions. The women glared at Hayden with undisguised contempt. After they supportively hugged Katie, they walked brusquely past him, fixing him with withering gazes.

He stood to greet her as she approached him. A scowl marred her brow, and fury simmered behind her deep blue eyes. Her long blonde hair, tied back in an efficient ponytail, enhanced her high cheekbones and graceful neck. Though she dressed conservatively, in a manner appropriate for her position, her lab coat did little to conceal her figure. He often said she would look sexy in coveralls.

"Why are you here, Hayden?"

"You didn't respond to any of my pings."

"You're surprised by that? You're unbelievable."

"I just wanted to explain—"

"What? What is there to explain? I caught you in bed with Sharon Ortega. The situation was fairly obvious to me."

"C'mon, Katie. I made a mistake. I'm sorry."

"A mistake, was it? No, Hayden, I think it is I who should make an apology to you."

"What?"

"Yes, I should apologize that I led you to think that any selfish thing you do is forgivable. It was an error on my part. I can't believe I put up with your bullshit for as long as I did."

He scowled. "Then why didn't you break up with me earlier? God knows I gave you enough reasons."

Her frown deepened. "I was too caught up with the status of being Hayden Kaine's girlfriend. I was enraptured by the mystique afforded you by your family's position. I was such a fool."

"Look, Katie. I messed up. I love you. I can change; get counselling; I can be a better person..."

"Kaine, you are an unbelievable asshole! You don't just decide to become your best self without changing something fundamental inside. Get your own life. The scripted existence you're living is going to be the end of you."

She stared at him while he searched for a response. As he struggled, her expression softened. She stood on her toes and kissed him on the cheek.

"Goodbye, Hayden. I hope you find what you need to wake up the man I know lives inside you."

She walked down the path and vanished into a building.

A ping to his cortical LINK snapped him from his trance. He tried to collect himself before accepting the message.

His initial surprise was replaced by excitement when he saw that it was from his father. That quickly turned to trepidation when he accessed the contents.

He was summoned to his father's office.

That was never an enjoyable experience.

The Admiral

HAYDEN'S THROAT WAS a parched desert, partly from the excessive amount of alcohol the previous night. The drip of perspiration running down the small of his back beneath his dress uniform convinced him that it was due to nerves.

He had only met Robert Thomas privately on two occasions; both encounters were uncomfortable, and this one was not shaping into anything more pleasant.

Ever since he read his summons to Geneva, he puzzled what this meeting could be about. His father's lack of insight had left him to stew about it for the hour-long trip to fleet headquarters.

Most cadets believed they were disliked by the Old Man, but Hayden was certain that the admiral hated him. From the stories floating around the campus, Thomas was well known for despising anyone who showed a passing interest in Katie Evans, his brilliant, attractive granddaughter. Hayden's fears were more than unfounded paranoia, especially given what had happened.

After an eternity of waiting, the secretarial synth entered the lounge and escorted him to the admiral's office. On wobbly legs, he followed the android toward the door. When it opened, he found them unwilling to obey his commands, leaving him standing in the entrance.

"Well, come in, please, Officer Cadet Kaine."

His feet finally responding to the invitation, he marched into the room and stood at attention before the most powerful man he knew; the one who would very soon determine the course of the rest of his military career, and the success or failure of his father's efforts.

Admiral Thomas stopped reading and regarded him. Hayden kept his eyes focused on a point above the Old Man's head and maintained textbook posture.

"At ease, Cadet. Please, take a seat."

Breaking eye contact with the wall, he tried to hide his incredulity. Obediently, he sat in the indicated chair, his back straight and not feeling at ease.

Thomas graced him with an amused smirk and returned his attention to what he had been reading. Finally, he put the smart paper down, placed both hands on either side of it, and fixed his gaze on the young cadet.

"I have followed your career with some interest. Given your involvement with Captain Evans, I'm sure you can appreciate why?"

Hayden swallowed hard and managed to squeak out his reply. "Yes, sir."

Another amused expression crossed the Old Man's face and he continued, "Your academic record at the academy is satisfactory enough." He picked up the document and referred to it as he spoke. "Most of your marks in military history, tactics, and strategy are adequate, but not exceptional. Your performance in the basic sciences is in the upper quartile, however. Due to the influence of my granddaughter, no doubt?"

Hayden nodded. "Yes, Admiral." There was no point now in revealing who was responsible for his success.

"Hmm. I thought as much." He returned to the transcript. "But your scores in political science and diplomacy are consistently at the top of the class."

"Yes, sir."

"Are you hoping to make a career for yourself with the diplomatic corps, Mister Kaine?"

Hayden paused at the leading question. His ambitions were well known to Katie who would undoubtedly have reported them to her grandfather. "I am, Admiral."

"That would explain the annoying and frequent communications from your father." Thomas fixed his full attention on him. He felt like a young rabbit caught in the gaze of a wolf contemplating how best to eat him.

"I don't respond well to influence peddling, Cadet. I am disposed to disdain for the young, privileged scions whose high-ranking parents think they can jump-start the career of their offspring through pandering."

The Old Man skewered him with a steady stare and Hayden counted off the seconds, waiting for the drop of the other shoe.

"I spent many long, sleepless nights considering how to assign you after your unavoidable graduation, Mister Kaine. Finally, something presented itself that serves multiple purposes for me."

Hayden braced himself in anticipation of what was coming.

"My personal preference is to send you to one of the outlying colonies for some minor posting, where I could ensure you were forgotten and forced to languish until retirement. It would be a satisfying answer to the entreaties of your father and get you away from my granddaughter."

Thomas let him digest that comment before continuing. "Fortunately for you, that sort of thing is frowned upon. Instead, I found another assignment that will get you out of my hair and actually serves a useful function."

Hayden felt the perspiration grow in his armpits and another trickle of sweat run down his lower back. He tried to imagine the worst possible posting the admiral could give him, coming up with several undesirable options.

Breaking the tension, the Old Man continued, appearing to enjoy the discomfort of his captive audience. "Effective immediately, I am graduating you from the academy and into the United Earth Forces with the commensurate rank of second lieutenant. You are to report to the Principal Orbital Space Dock at 0900 GMT for transfer to the UEF cruiser, *Scimitar*. There you will assume your post under the command of Captain Yegor Pavlovich."

Thomas stood and extended his right hand over the desk. Stunned, Hayden rose and accepted the firm handshake, then saluted his commanding officer.

"Your ship's formal mission parameters will be released to you once you arrive on the *Scimitar*. Godspeed, Mister Kaine."

Realizing that he was now dismissed, he said, "Thank you, Admiral."

As he walked to the doorway, Thomas called out to him, "Please don't try to contact my granddaughter to say your goodbyes. I believe she does not wish to hear from you, based on my conversations with her."

He swallowed hard. "Yes, sir."

Exiting the office, he made his way to the lobby, not sure what his fate was.

"COME IN, SON. DO YOU want a drink?"

Hayden's father was tall and lean, without a grey strand in his full head of hair. It was tied back in a chonmage, typical for men of his social and political status.

"No, thanks," said Hayden as he collapsed into an armchair.

Walden Kaine's office was more like the smoking room of a nineteenth century men's club. A faux bookshelf concealed the desk, and the room was decorated in priceless antique furniture.

"Well, I'm having one."

He walked to the bar and selected a single malt for himself. Hayden winced when his father added ice. Despite his position and influence, the man had never learned how to take his whisky.

After savouring his first sip, he sat opposite his son beside the fireplace. Holographic flames snapped and threw off too much heat for Hayden's comfort.

He scowled as his father made a show of enjoying the expensive liquor he couldn't possibly appreciate. The man could be drinking kerosene and not know the difference.

"I heard that Iris took a turn for the worse. I'm sorry, son."

His consoling tone grated on Hayden's nerves.

"Why am I here, Dad?"

"Do I need a reason to want to see you?"

He stared at his father through narrowed eyelids.

The older man shrugged. "I learned today that Admiral Thomas summoned you. Do you know why?"

He was not surprised his father knew more about his life than he had any right to. He'd long ago abandoned any illusions of privacy where Walden Kaine was concerned.

"No, but I thought you might, by the tone of your message."

"No. The Old Man hasn't returned my calls. I can only assume it is for something significant. Not many cadets are summoned to Geneva. One of my connections probably reached Thomas where I couldn't."

Hayden needed a drink, but he dared not show up in Thomas's office with booze on his breath.

"I wish you didn't push so hard..."

"Are you still on that 'I want to do it myself' shit? Grow up, son. You need to exploit every advantage available to you. It is the only way we can keep things on schedule."

"I realize that. God knows you lecture me often enough about my 'destiny.'"

Walden frowned. "Well, then don't muck it up." His expression softened, and he raised his glass in a toast. "Congratulations, Hayden. I'm proud of you."

"I didn't do anything to be congratulated for."

"That is your girlfriend talking. She doesn't know anything about politics. Do you think she got to her position on her own merit? Wake up! She's Thomas's granddaughter."

"Katie is brilliant in her own right. She would be where she is without her family's connections."

"You can try to delude yourself about that, but we both know you can't rely solely on your own abilities. Nothing about your time at the academy has distinguished you. Without my help, you'll end up as some junior officer on a ship posted...who knows where? That is a dead-end career that will do none of us any good."

"Especially not you. Isn't that right, Dad?"

"This has nothing to do with me. I did my part. Now it's your turn. Don't screw things up."

Hayden shifted in the overstuffed chair. Abruptly, he stood. "I should go, or I'll miss my shuttle to Geneva."

Walden rose, extending his hand. "Of course. Good luck, son."

He hesitated, at a loss for what to say. Everything that came to mind seemed trite and insincere. How many times had he told himself that he was done with his father, only to swallow his petty rebellions and return to what was expected of him?

He would have turned his back on Walden Kaine years ago, if not for Iris's insistence he honour his father. She was old-fashioned that way.

So, with her in mind, he swallowed his petulant pride, forced himself to smile, and did the least offensive thing possible.

He accepted his father's hand.

What other choice was there?

Beginning and End

THE CONTRACTED PERSONNEL transfer ship must have been twenty years past its best-before date. Its ancient light-gate engines took eighteen hours to recharge between jumps. Consequently, it took five days to make the required FTL hops to the Zeta Tucanae system. By the time they arrived, Hayden needed a shower and a change of scene to anything but the interior of the *Antares*. He was positive the admiral had assigned him to this vessel on purpose. Any of the newer ships of the fleet could make the trip in twenty hours.

The ship was berthed in the run-down civilian wing of the station. The facility, while clean, smelled of a faint combination of mold and disinfectant.

Hayden's LINK connected to the local OM-NET node and he reviewed the messages awaiting his attention. His heart almost stopped when he saw one from Penny, the nurse at the palliative care unit.

While her message was compassionate, her carefully chosen words could not blunt their impact.

Iris had died while Hayden was in transit.

Walden Kaine had made the funeral arrangements and held in trust Iris's bequest to him.

With tear-filled eyes, he scrolled through the other messages, searching for something from his father. On finding it, he paused before opening it, afraid of what it might contain.

He didn't really know his father. The man was absent for most of Hayden's childhood. Only when he'd reached his teen years did circumstances change and Walden attempt to build a relationship between them.

He was certain that it was Iris who was behind his almost herculean effort. Whether she had coached him or not, Hayden couldn't say, but the work bore some fruit, because they were at least on speaking terms.

Swallowing the lump in his throat, he accessed the message.

Walden Kaine said all the right words. In fact, they were beautifully written. The problem was they were too perfect. The man was ever the consummate politician and a skilled wordsmith, practiced at writing copy to expertly elicit whatever reaction served his purpose.

Hayden was sure some level of sincerity lay within the subtext of the missive. His father was not heartless. She was as much a friend to him as she had been to his dead wife.

Hayden located a small cafe and occupied a quiet table in the corner where he could go unnoticed. There, in a strange place, where nobody knew him or saw him, he wept.

When his tears would no longer flow, he sat back and imagined what she might say about his emotional display.

She would tell him, *Tosh-tosh, young man. Everyone dies. It is a part of the journey. Mourn, yes, but do not let sorrow shape your life. Dead is dead, and there is no number of tears or wishing that can change that. Have your cry, say your goodbyes, and move on, keeping happy memories of your time with them.*

He wiped his eyes. "Goodbye."

HAYDEN DECIDED WORK would be the balm for sorrow. Though he spent most of the trip dreading his new assignment, it was time to do what Iris would tell him to do. The fitting way to remember and honour her was to put forth his best effort in whatever personal hell Admiral Thomas had prepared for him.

After locating an information synth, he learned the berth number of *Scimitar* and made his way through several security stations into the military wing of the aging facility.

Holding his small bag, he stood before airlock door 563 and tried to, if not stop the butterflies in his stomach, at least persuade them to fly in formation.

Hayden was shocked from his thoughts by a woman's voice.

"The inside of the ship smells a lot better than out here."

He turned to see a petite young blonde woman wearing filthy coveralls. The left side of her head was shaved, and an elaborate glyph of some kind was tattooed on the exposed scalp. Her remaining hair was long and pulled back into a semblance of a military-approved ponytail.

"You *are* looking for the *Scimitar*, aren't you?"

"Uh, yes," he stammered. "I'm Second Lieutenant Kaine."

She broke into a grin. "Ooo, the brand-new officer, straight from the factory."

She wiped her right hand on her coverall and extended it to him. "I'm Midshipman Cora Symes, Engineer's Mate, though there isn't actually an official engineer. I guess that makes me one, though I'm not commissioned, so they can't give me that title. Not that titles matter much on this ship."

He couldn't help but smile at her, and, with only a slight hesitation, took her offered hand and they shook.

"I'm pleased to meet you, Midshipman Symes."

"Oh, everyone calls me Cora."

He grinned even wider at her rapid speech. "That sounds good. You can call me Hayden."

She seized his bag from his other hand. Before he could object, she walked past him and opened the airlock door.

"The cap'n will be mighty glad to see you. We've been waiting three days and were beginning to think you wouldn't arrive. Headquarters often doesn't follow through with what they tell us."

"They sent me by the slow boat."

"Oh, no worries. You're here now, and that's what counts. We are a bit understaffed in the officer department. Actually, we pretty much need more people everywhere, though I was lucky enough to get two additional junior engineering techs last month."

Was she pulling his leg? Why would HQ allow a ship of the line to be neglected like this?

She smiled at the look of shock on his face. "Not too many want to serve a tour on the frontier. Things aren't nearly as exciting or civilized as the inner systems, but I like it."

"I'm afraid they didn't give me a choice."

"Your first assignment. I get it. Don't worry, I doubt the cap'n would leave you behind, no matter what he threatened. Only his bark is mean, and he hardly ever bites. Besides, there are still repairs to make on the gravity plating and some tuning of the light-gate drive, so we won't be going anywhere for another day anyway."

She grinned at him while Hayden remained in the airlock, fascinated by how she could fit so much speech into a single breath.

"He's waiting for you now."

"Who?"

"Cap'n Pavlovich. He's on the bridge." She pointed to her left. "Just go that way, through three hatches and down the last ladder. I put the sign back up yesterday. If you get lost, ask anyone."

Hayden looked at his bag in her hand.

"Unless you want me to take you there?" she said.

"Uh, no, that's okay. I'm sure I'll find my way."

"Yeah, that's what I thought. You look like a smart one. I'm heading past your quarters on my way to engineering, so I'll drop your kit off. See you at mealtime."

She abruptly turned and disappeared through a hatchway.

Shaking his head, he turned in the opposite direction, and, with little difficulty, found himself outside the hatch to the command hub. He was debating if he should knock first or simply enter when it swung open on its own.

Standing, hunched over in the doorway, was a startled bear of a man. He was easily over two metres tall, and his rumpled uniform couldn't conceal a muscular body. His pale, lined face was covered in an unkempt jet-black beard, while his head was shorn. Dark brown eyes glared from beneath bushy black eyebrows.

"Who the hell are you?" His voice was loud and threatening.

Hayden noted the rank epaulette on the man's collar and realized this was Yegor Pavlovich, commanding officer of the *Scimitar*. He snapped to attention and saluted.

"Second Lieutenant Kaine reporting for duty as ordered, sir."

The captain stared at him, betraying no emotion. "Well, it's about time. Come in." He retreated through the hatchway.

Hayden self-consciously ended his salute and followed.

Pavlovich towered beside him and gave him several seconds to take in the scene of the small, cramped bridge of the ship. Everyone stopped what they were doing and gawked at him.

"Attention! Our new monkey from Central Command has arrived. Mister...er..."

"Kaine, sir."

"Right. Anyway, he is your new first officer. Fill him in."

"Sir?"

Annoyance clouded Pavlovich's brow. "Some of my crew are in the station's stockade, making us more understaffed than normal. You are now the second ranking officer aboard, and, by default, my XO. I am going to take a dump, so these fine people will bring you up to speed on your duties. I will see you in the ship's mess in one hour, where we will share a meal and open our orders."

He started to depart but abruptly reconsidered and moved closer to Hayden. Speaking quietly, he said, "You stink. Get a shower before supper."

Without waiting for a response, Pavlovich exited and slammed the hatchway shut behind him. The newly minted executive officer turned back to the bridge crew, who had resumed their previous activities.

What the hell kind of ship am I assigned to?

The Mission

DEBRIEFED ON HIS GENERAL duties and operational procedure, meaning how the captain liked things done, Hayden retreated to his quarters to clean up properly for the first time in almost a week.

His cabin was small but had its own tiny shower. As the tepid waters ran over him, he reflected on what he had gotten himself into. Except for the travel arrangements, this didn't feel like a punitive assignment. Perhaps the news about Iris had coloured his perception.

As he dried himself, he resolved to take a more positive view of his situation and put his best foot forward. It was the most fitting way he could honour her. This posting was not how his father imagined Hayden's career might begin, but it could be a significant step in the right direction, if he played it right.

He dressed in his clean uniform and found his way to the mess hall. Pavlovich insisted that the crew dine together every evening while in space dock. On reflection, he could see the wisdom in building camaraderie that way. He might learn a lot before the end of the mission.

The door opened to reveal what he presumed was the ship's complement. Sixty-two men and women, with untouched plates piled with food before them, stared at him with barely concealed resentment behind their eyes; everyone except for Cora, who regarded him with pity and shook her head, as if embarrassed for him.

Checking his LINK, he noted he was thirty-five seconds late and wondered what the problem could be. Under everyone's gaze, he self-consciously proceeded to the serving station and piled random items on his tray. With every eye in the room following, he took the only remaining seat across from the captain. As soon as he sat, Pavlovich seized his fork and dove into his meal like a man who hadn't eaten in a week. Everyone else followed suit, and the room was filled with the sounds of scraped plates and noisy chewing. Every person was focused on the plate in front of them. Hayden spooned food into his mouth, unsure if a social penalty existed for being the last to finish.

As he chewed the final mouthful, he became aware he was again being watched. He looked up to see Pavlovich sternly gazing at him. His plate was empty, and his utensils lay on it. Hayden roughly swallowed and placed his cutlery down. He glanced about to note that every other person appeared to be finished as well, and all waited for him.

Seeming satisfied that everyone was done, Pavlovich stood to address the assembled crew. "I'm glad that you all could make it for supper." He shot a glance at Hayden. "As I'm sure you are all aware, we will be running a bit light on personnel, as Commander Pierce and Lieutenant Watkins and a few others elected to remain behind and enjoy the hospitality of the docking station security forces."

Chuckles rose from the back of the room, and the captain tried to suppress a smile.

"Regardless of their inconsiderate absence from the family, we are graced with a new arrival. Some of you met Lieutenant Kaine earlier, and the rest of you will get to know him and form your own opinion as he assumes the role of first officer. I expect you to give him the same degree of respect that you accorded Mister Pierce."

He raised a data pad and read from it. "Effective immediately, *Scimitar* is ordered to proceed by fastest practical jump sequence to the Mu Arae system. There we are to locate and recover Doctor Ishmael Gabriel and return him and his accumulated research to Earth, posthaste."

Pavlovich raised his eyes and scowled at the mumbling crew. "Is there something anyone would like to share?" He scanned the now quiet room and pointed at a young crewman near the back wall who was trying to avoid his gaze.

"You, Brennen. You seemed particularly talkative a moment ago while I was speaking. What do you wish to say?"

The man sitting beside Cora hesitantly stood and addressed Pavlovich. "Cap'n, Mu Arae has been off the light grid for the past forty years. We don't know if the light-gate even works anymore."

"I heard it does," interrupted another voice. "Raiders hacked it and use it for smuggling. They're in league with the aliens who destroyed the colony and will attack any ship that attempts to enter the system. The *Odin* barely made it back when they tried to go in ten years ago."

A rumble of assent rose in the room. Pavlovich scowled at his assembled crew.

"What the hell is the matter with you pansies? Who pays attention to any of the crap that is floating around the OM-NET? You all have too much recreation time. *Odin* was a class two scout ship with no weapons and was attacked *before* they could make the jump. My grandmother's knitting circle could have commandeered it."

He glared at the crowd. "The rumours about Mu Arae are just that. There are no alien bogeymen. The colony failed due to nothing more sinister than a natural disaster. Forget what other crap you may have heard. "As far as raiders are concerned, need I remind everyone that *Scimitar* is an armed cruiser with a trained fighting crew? At least, that is what I say in the reports I file. We've taken on our fair share of pirates, and they always came out the worse for it. What is really going on here?"

The room fell silent, and several people glanced at Hayden, who felt increasingly uncomfortable with their attention. Pavlovich noticed the dynamic in the room. His eyes widened mockingly.

"Oh, I see what the problem is. You lot don't feel confident about going into a potential conflict situation with our crew complement down and a green XO."

The murmurs in the room grew, and a few heads nodded.

"Listen up, you whiners! Yes, we are an out-of-date ship on crap duty at the rump end of the Confederation. Yes, most of you are here because I was the last commander prepared to accept you, and some of you may even think that I am out of favour with the powers that be. Get over it. Despite what you think of this vessel, your crew mates, or me, this is still a ship of the line and you are all enlisted and paid by the United Earth Forces to defend its goddamned territories and interests."

Buzzing from the overhead light seemed to boom in Hayden's ears. Somebody coughed.

"I am appointing Lieutenant Kaine as XO. That should be good enough for you. Mister Pierce broke the law and is in jail now, so unless you want to jump ship, my advice is to stow the mumbling and prepare to depart at 0600. Dismissed!"

Everyone filed past the recycling unit, where they dumped their plates as they exited the mess hall. Not a word was spoken.

Pavlovich regarded his still seated first officer. "The crew does not appear to trust you yet, Mister Kaine. I don't know if I do either, but you're all Command gave me, so I am willing to give you enough rope to hang yourself. I assigned you a provisional field promotion to full lieutenant. I don't know if you're worthy of it, and frankly, I don't care. I did it to piss off the Old Man. It's up to you to keep it."

After a beat to see if he would reply, the captain continued. "It would appear you have some work to do, XO. Oversee preparations for departure."

Hayden stood and saluted. "Aye-aye, sir!"

Pavlovich shook his head with a pained expression. "Knock off the saluting. Wake me at 0500."

Discarding his plate in the recycling unit, he stomped out, leaving Hayden more confused than ever.

HAYDEN WAS SURE PAVLOVICH was trying to kill him on the Old Man's orders. The demands of his position were exhausting. The captain claimed the punishing schedule was necessary because of the reduced crew complement and the number of jumps required to get them to their objective. Only when the aging engines failed on the approach to the final gate did he reluctantly agree everyone was exhausted and ordered most of them to bed.

Hayden wondered if that order had included Cora. The young engineer seemed to thrive on the pressure. As far as he knew, she took no downtime. He suspected she kept a supply of stimms and considered asking if she would share with him.

No sooner would she and her team put one thing back online than another system would fail. Artificial gravity went out three times, and they lost life support in half the lower decks at one point.

Hayden worried they would never make it back to Earth, marooned somewhere or dying in an explosion when something critical failed.

One jump-gate remained to be traversed. It was perhaps fortuitous that they now had some time to put the ship in good order before making the final FTL leap into the unknown.

Still exhausted, despite a brief opportunity for sleep, he arrived for his shift on the bridge thirty seconds ahead of schedule. He even had enough time to grab a cup of strong coffee from the mess hall.

Pavlovich looked up from the command chair to acknowledge his arrival. Hayden noted two officers were already at their posts and well into preparations for activation of the light-gate drive. Ensign Bates, a rail-thin albino man of indeterminate age, was at the sensor and communications console. Ensign Kwok, a petite Asian woman of about forty years, occupied the helm/navigation station.

Two stations remained unoccupied: engineering control and the tactical alcove, an isolated booth for the ship's gunnery commander. That bridge position alone dated the vessel to a time before all ship defences became managed by synths.

Hayden immediately logged himself in, and, one by one, verified his interlink with each system. It had taken him a couple of days beyond his initial orientation to become comfortable with *Scimitar's* archaic interfaces.

"Engineer, report please?" Pavlovich spoke into an ancient headset. It was another anachronism Hayden needed to get used to.

He glanced up and noted the engineering station was empty.

"Well, get it finished and haul your ass up here." The captain removed the apparatus and as an afterthought addressed Kaine. "She's patching a coolant leak and will be right up."

He nodded his thanks and silently wondered how the ship had survived so long out at the fringes.

Eight minutes later, Cora breezed in, unfazed, and assumed her station. After logging in, she announced, almost incidentally, "All systems are green for FTL jump, Cap'n."

"About bloody time." He regarded the still open hatchway.

"Where the hell is Gunney?"

She smiled at Pavlovich. "He's coming, sir. Don't worry."

"I thought I met the entire bridge crew," said Hayden.

"He is our tactical officer, Kaine. He doesn't much like hanging out with the rest of us."

"He's been down in engineering getting updated," added Cora.

"He's a synth?"

The captain laughed. "Don't ever let him hear you call him that."

"He's a cyborg," Cora said. "Gunney doesn't like people much."

Hayden was dumbfounded. It figured that the *Scimitar* had an outdated gunnery officer. Before he could say anything, a rhythmic clanking echoed through the open hatch and an enormous hulk of a man lurched through it. He slammed the door shut and made his way to his station.

"Gunney, how many times do I have to tell you to take it easy on my ship? We just fixed that," said Pavlovich, not unkindly, to the man's back.

A raspy voice that sounded like sandpaper being scraped across a microphone responded, "Sorry, Cap'n."

The cyborg assumed his position inside the alcove.

Kaine caught himself staring and broke off his gaze. He'd never met a cybernetic enhanced person before and only knew of them through his history class. Gunney showed few external signs of his prosthesis, and Hayden couldn't tell how much of the man was still human. He assumed from the awkward clanking of his gait that his lower body was synthetic and reinforced to military specs. Aside from that, except for the metallic voice and an obvious artificial left eye, he appeared to be an unusually large man.

Pavlovich settled into his command chair. "I believe we are now all present and ready. Initiate the jump, Mister Kaine."

"Aye, sir. Helm, bring us to full zero motion relative to the light-gate."

After verifying on his own station that all systems were green, Hayden said, "Awaiting your authorization sequence sir."

The captain entered the access code on his console.

"Codes accepted by gate control. We are authorized to transit," said Bates.

"Roger that," said Cora. "Spinning up light-gate drive. Maximum power available in twenty seconds." Her eyes were riveted to the redundant console readouts at her station.

Following the requisite delay, she announced, "Drives at full spin. We are go across the board."

Mindful of all the various rumours about what awaited them on the other side, Hayden swallowed hard and prayed his voice would not crack. "Initiate FTL transit."

The sensation of a jump was something he had never been able to get used to. The only way he could ever manage to describe it was to say that the world winked out for a moment. A slight dizziness was the only residual effect he experienced.

According to the readings, they were in the Mu Arae system, 100 kilometres from its own light-gate.

"Jump completed, Captain," he said. "All systems read as normal." The information was available on their implants, but Pavlovich insisted on verbal confirmation of status.

"Long range scans?"

"Actively scanning, sir. No contacts," said Bates. Moments later, the pitch of his voice rose. "Correction. Bogie contact, 100,000 kilometres off the port bow."

The exact coordinates flashed up in Hayden's implant.

"Identification? Size and vector. Give me something," said Pavlovich.

"No ID beacon. Configuration: small recon drone. Heading parallels our own."

"Raiders?" asked Hayden.

The captain nodded. "We've seen these things before. Ensign, is it sending out any communications?"

"No comm detected, sir, but I began jamming the moment we spotted her."

The corners of Pavlovich's mouth curled upward. "Gunney, I don't want that thing telling its pals about us."

"Already on it, Cap'n," rasped the tactical officer.

Hayden followed on his LINK as the ship's port bow rail gun array targeted the drone. The firing solution flashed up the same moment the rumbling deck plates told him they'd fired. Seconds later, in concert with his implant readout, Gunney announced, "Target neutralized."

"Thank you, Tactical. Any further contacts, Mister Bates?"

"None, sir. I'm getting intermittent static on the dorsal stern sensor array, though."

Pavlovich frowned at Cora.

"I'll get right on it, Cap'n." She rose from her station and exited.

"All right, people. So far, nothing out of the ordinary, so either the bogeymen are asleep, or they don't exist. Deploy proximity drones for maximum coverage."

He turned to Hayden, a mischievous glint in his eye. "Let's go see if we can find the scientist Command is so hot about. Set our heading for Dulcinea at best speed."

"Aye, Captain," he replied, now fully awake.

Mu Arae

TWENTY HOURS LATER, *Scimitar* approached Dulcinea. Hayden had not left his post during the transit to the inner system. He spent the time obsessively checking preliminary data summaries for any sign of another vessel with more hostile intentions than the destroyed bogie.

As with many things aboard, the orbital sensors were outdated. Still, he was impressed by the customized upgrades Cora built into the drones to modernize them. Fifty-five tiny robotic craft circled *Scimitar* at variable distances, each feeding multiple channels of data back to the ship.

"Mister Kaine, we are now getting high-resolution imagery of Dulcinea," said Bates, who also had not taken a break since arrival in the system.

On the three-dimensional viewer at the front of the bridge, a life-like hologram of the planet, still fifteen million kilometres away, resolved.

The world was a hellish wasteland. No part of it was untouched by the lava flows that erupted from a major impact site defacing its surface. Dulcinea's once Earth-like atmosphere was gone, blasted away in the cataclysm. The once teeming seas had boiled off in a matter of days. The emptied ocean basins were filled with the molten rock that belched from a global chain of ruptured tectonic plate boundaries.

Above it, in random decaying orbits, were the remains of the defensive fleet that fought in vain to protect the colony world, the spinning debris flashing in the sunlight. The crew stared, speechless at the slowly rotating image.

"Nothing could be alive down there," said Hayden.

"According to the original rescue ships, nothing is," said Pavlovich, who had joined him, unnoticed. "It looks pretty much the same as the images recorded by the *Titan*. Those poor bastards couldn't do a thing. By the time they made orbit, the attackers were gone."

"How many survivors were there?" asked Cora.

The captain shook his head, never taking his eyes from the image. "There weren't any."

"Nobody?" She wiped tears away.

"I don't think there is any point going to the planet," said Pavlovich. "Our missing scientist couldn't survive down there. Where else might Dr. Gabriel be hiding?"

Hayden said, "Sir, I analyzed the sensor logs from our encounter with the drone. It received a short, encoded signal before we jammed it."

"Is there a fix on where it originated?"

Kaine nodded. "The system's asteroid belt."

The captain smiled. "There was a mining operation in place there forty-years ago. *Titan* evacuated them, but if others still hang about, it would provide a place for them to live."

"It would be a perfect base of operations for raiders, sir."

The captain regarded Hayden and raised an eyebrow. "Are you afraid of some scruffy pirates? We are a warship, Mister Kaine."

He smiled. "Aye, Captain. Helm, plot a course to the source of the transmission."

As Kwok executed the command, Pavlovich said, "Anything else of interest come up during your watch, XO?"

He frowned. "Rear viewing sensors are still experiencing intermittent static."

"Really? Cora couldn't fix it?"

"She reports that all drones are working up to specs. It might be coming from the light-gate back there."

Pavlovich seemed distracted when he replied, "I'm sure it is something like that. Nobody has been around to run maintenance on it for a long time. Still..."

"Sir?"

"Keep an eye on it as we change course."

"You think we're being followed? Nothing is showing up on any sensor channel. We're running the full electromagnetic spectrum."

"I think we're going to be very cautious, Lieutenant. Whoever attacked Dulcinea all those years ago managed to surprise everyone. Who's to say they all left? Three warships disappeared in this system since then."

"Those stories are true?"

"Just watch the sensors, XO."

"Aye, Captain."

Hayden wondered if doing radiation or sewage maintenance would be such a bad assignment after all.

A Pursuer

SCIMITAR was five hours into what was supposed to be a four-hour transit. The mining facility, Friston VI, was constructed on the largest asteroid in the belt. The captain had insisted Kwok plot a wandering course to their destination. Though none of their communication hails were answered, they maintained the meandering path. They simply had no other leads for where to begin looking for the scientist, Ishmael Gabriel.

The intermittent static continued astern of them, so Pavlovich ordered additional turns to their heading to give the ship's drones a chance to triangulate an origin for the interference. Hayden constantly monitored the processing output of the sensor analysis.

"Sir, the bugs detect a source beyond the maximal ones out at 1,000 kilometres. Can we extend their orbital range? Maybe we can get it within their orbits and narrow down a location."

Pavlovich turned toward the engineering station. "How about it, Cora? How far out can you push the bugs?"

"Well..." she drawled with a slight upward curl on her lips, "I tinkered with the software a while back to let them move out to ten thousand klicks from the ship, but it isn't tested yet. This might be a good opportunity."

"You won't lose any of them, like the last time? It took me months to get replacements authorized."

"That was not my fault, sir. You decided to do a light-gate jump before I could retrieve them all. No, Cap'n, that won't happen. Can I try it? I have been dying for a chance."

"Yes, Engineer, you may proceed with your test."

"Whee!" squealed Cora like a teenager. She spun her chair to face her console and brought up a keyboard on it. Hayden raised his eyebrow and looked at Pavlovich.

"Believe it or not, Kaine, she can program faster using that ancient interface than any other engineer with their implant. She is a bit of a savant that way."

"Aww, Cap'n," said Cora without looking up from her station, "you say the sweetest things. You're gonna make me blush in front of our XO."

Pavlovich smiled at her, which surprised Hayden, who had to date not seen him show any kind of favouritism toward anyone. He hesitated with what he realized was an impertinent question dangling on the tip of his tongue. The captain frowned at him.

"You want to say something, Kaine?"

He was rescued by an announcement from Cora. "Okay, bugs' orbital range is now extended to ten thousand klicks astern. I adjusted the search parameters to triangulate a position of the source, but it won't be precise."

Pavlovich did not hide his annoyance. "How approximate?"

"Positioning error of plus or minus one hundred metres, which isn't a problem if it's really, really huge." She shrugged and grinned sheepishly. Hayden smiled back at her and began to monitor the output from the new configuration.

"Thank you, Engineer," said the captain. "Bates, any luck on raising a response from the mining facility?"

"Still nothing, Cap'n."

"Hmph," grumbled Pavlovich as he slumped into his chair. A moment later, he straightened and addressed Hayden.

"Oh, by the way, that was a good idea you had about extending the bugs' range. Keep up the acceptable work."

He suppressed a smile. "Yes, sir."

The bridge fell into silence as everyone focused their attention on their tasks. It was evident that the cause of the static bursts had followed them. Hayden was glad of Pavlovich's presence. Left on his own, he might have been tempted to order Bates to try to establish communications with whatever was out there. For the second time since his arrival, he conceded this assignment was a beneficial learning opportunity.

"It looks like the repositioning worked, Captain. We are getting location information for the interference source," he said.

"Uh-oh!"

Pavlovich sat forward in his chair and turned to glare at the engineer. "What's uh-oh? I hate uh-oh, Cora. Fix it."

Her fingers flew over her keyboard. "I don't think I can, Cap'n. We've lost telemetry with the light-gate."

"What? Is the problem on this end?"

"No, sir. It simply stopped returning our pings. I'm trying to restore contact with it now, but I get no response."

"Light-gates don't do that, Cora. There are redundancies on top of contingencies."

"Well, getting mad at me won't help. This one *did* stop talking to us."

Pavlovich scowled at her for a moment, before turning to Hayden. "XO, what were you saying about the static source?"

"It is 5,060 kilometres astern, give or take."

He continued to monitor the results on his implant when his eyes widened in surprise. "And it appears to be closing on us."

"ACTION STATIONS!" ORDERED the captain.

The bridge lighting dimmed, replaced by red, night-vision illumination.

"Helm, accelerate to point 15 c. Heading: toward the nearest rock in the asteroid belt."

"Targeting data is being forwarded to tactical," said Hayden, unable to suppress the stress in his voice.

"Estimates, XO?"

"Our triangulation is preliminary, sir. I think they figured out what we were up to and made their move before we could nail down their position."

"Hmph. We got caught with our pants down." The captain rotated his chair to address the tactical officer. "Gunney, is there a firing solution computed?"

"No precise positioning info, Cap'n, but there is enough for a spread of laser fire with a good chance of hitting home."

Pavlovich looked sternly at Hayden. "Now I only need to decide if I'm going to shoot first. What does your fancy academy education suggest, XO?"

Perspiration ran down Hayden's cheek. His only exposure to this type of situation had been simulations, and he had never performed well in them.

He addressed Bates. "Comm, is there any kind of signal from astern? Any sign they are trying to hail us?"

"Not a peep, Lieutenant."

Hayden returned Pavlovich's dark, angry stare, then decided. "Their actions are provocative, sir. I recommend we fire."

"It took you long enough. Okay, Gunney, give it to 'em."

The lighting on the bridge dimmed further, and *Scimitar*'s hull vibrated as the ship's stern array of twelve, 500-exawatt X-ray lasers fired at their pursuer. The barrage continued for twenty-seconds before stopping to allow the weapons to recharge.

"Status of target?" asked the captain.

"No indications of impact, energy discharge, or debris."

"You mean we missed?"

"Not bloody likely, sir," said Gunney.

The ship lurched and the pull of the gravity plating weakened. The lights winked out, and only emergency illumination prevented them from plunging into total darkness.

"Status report!" said Pavlovich.

Hayden futilely tried to access his disconnected implant.

Cora's hands flew across the manual interface at her station, and she scrutinized the readouts. "We've been damaged astern. Engine two is inoperative, and number four is barely hanging on. Attitude control is offline...give me a second." Her fingers danced over the keyboard, and a moment later Hayden felt himself being pushed sideways by an invisible force. He grabbed the captain's console to steady himself.

"Okay, attitude control reestablished."

The hull hummed again with another barrage of laser fire. Pavlovich turned expectantly to Gunney, who shook his head.

"How the hell did you miss?"

Anger flared in Gunney's human eye. "There is no bloody way I missed, Cap'n. The lasers ain't touching them."

Cora examined her readouts in more detail. "No hull breach, but magnetic plating didn't do much to stop whatever they hit us with. We've got a lot of structural damage on ventral decks six through nine."

"Evacuate all noncritical personnel to the central core. Clear the compromised sections and vent whichever ones are unoccupied. I don't want any explosive decompressions."

Pavlovich activated ship-wide address. "All hands: prep for possible zero-g battle conditions." He addressed Cora. "I didn't like how the plating responded to that last hit, Engineer."

"Yes, sir, I'm doing my best but..." She shook her head.

"Analysis. What the hell did they use on us?"

With his link to no longer talking to ship's systems, Hayden had migrated to an unoccupied console and strapped himself into the chair.

"Whatever it was didn't register with the bugs."

The ship was rocked a second time. Hayden's stomach lurched as the pull of gravity vanished.

Cora called out a litany of damages. "Power to grav-plating is out; damage to stern laser array elements six through eight; aft rail gun is destroyed; structural breaches on decks nine and ten; engines four and three and two offline..."

"I need a solution, people!"

Hayden shouted above the noise, "Captain, the fact that we can't see them, and our lasers don't affect them..."

Pavlovich stared at him. "Well? Go on?"

He swallowed then said, "Try using projectile weapons. Fire a volley as they approach us; they'll be within one hundred klicks in fifteen seconds."

"Our aft array is gone, boy!" said Gunney.

"Attitude control is functional. Bring us around and present our forward guns," said Kaine.

"Helm, do it!" said Pavlovich.

The cyborg returned his attention to his tactical console. Hayden felt himself pulled sideways as Kwok rotated the ship to face the invisible attacker. Before the rotational movement stopped, the sound and shaking of the forward rail gun being unleashed vibrated the deck.

Anxious, he monitored the sensor drone readouts for any indication of an impact.

"We hit them!" he shouted. "Registered three hits. Some damage, I think. I read gas venting. They are breaking off and heading away from us."

A cheer arose on the bridge from everyone except Pavlovich.

"Where did they go, Kaine?"

"They accelerated and left our drone range at high speed. We've lost them."

"Great, so we only hurt them. Who knows when they'll come back and maybe bring reinforcements?"

"Cap'n, we've got some serious damage repairs to make," said Cora.

He nodded at her, and she unbuckled herself and floated to the hatchway.

"We're going to need a place to hide while we repair ourselves and come up with a plan of action," said the captain.

"Aye, sir," said Hayden, eyes still trained on the screen in front of him. "I think we're too far from the mining colony under our present condition, but I found us somewhere to lie low. There is a debris field 100,000 klicks to our port. We might be able to power down and float among the wreckage until we are repaired. Hopefully it will mask our signature from...whoever they are."

"What kind of wreck, Mister Kaine?"

"It looks like the remains of a UEF heavy cruiser, sir."

"Great, now we are going to hide from the monsters in a graveyard." Pavlovich drummed his fingers on the arm of his chair. "Kwok; set course for it. Best speed."

Hayden reexamined the sensor logs, praying he wasn't sending them into something worse.

Hide and Repair

THE JOURNEY TO THE wrecked ship took several hours. Unwilling to leave an energy trail for their attackers to follow, the captain ordered all but essential power shut down. Though it risked making them blind, the bugs were retrieved as well. Their remaining engine was pulsed once, then deactivated to let inertia carry *Scimitar* to the debris field.

"Okay, people," announced Pavlovich, "now is the time to earn your pay. What is our distance to that wreck?"

"We are just inside of five thousand klicks, Cap'n," replied Kwok.

"Marvellous. Mister Kaine, please deploy the sensor drones."

"I already launched them, sir."

Hayden's blood froze when Pavlovich's gaze bored into him, a critical eyebrow raised. After a few seconds of focussing withering attention on him, the captain said impatiently, "Well, what are they seeing?"

"There are low-level EM emissions from the largest section of the ship."

"Are they strong enough to mask our signature?"

"If we shut down all nonessential systems, I believe so."

"Some luck, finally. This plan may not be such a harebrained idea after all, Kaine." A subtle smile, mostly concealed by his beard, curled up the edge of Pavlovich's mouth.

Gravity plating still not functional, Cora floated to peer at the readout over Hayden's shoulder. Despite the dominant smell of grease on her skin, he could detect a faint residual scent of lavender.

"That section is still intact, and our sensors show infrared hot spots," she said. "Life support might still be active aboard."

"You mean survivors? How long has this ship been here?"

"Three warships were sent into this system a year after the attack and were never heard from again," said Pavlovich. "This wreck has to be one of them, so almost forty years. I can't imagine how any of the crew could be alive."

"Raiders, then?"

"Well, they won't be a problem to us if they're forced to live like this. Any more of those static emissions?"

Hayden shook his head. "Nothing detected."

Cora floated over to the captain's command chair.

"Cap'n, raiders or not, that section of wreckage could save our asses. I can scavenge a lot of what I need to repair our damage."

"Assuming it wasn't stripped bare decades ago."

She smiled. "You forget what I can do with junk parts, sir."

Pavlovich returned her smile. "Okay, Cora. We'll play it your way. Assemble your teams. But they aren't going in until the place is swept. Gunney, prep a tac team. I want every cubic centimetre of that wreck cleared by your Rangers."

"Aye-aye, Cap'n."

He faced Hayden. "Time for the training wheels to come off, Mister Kaine." He made no attempt to hide his amusement. "I'm putting you in charge of the sweep mission."

Gunney glared at the equally surprised XO.

Was the captain out of his mind? He had access to Hayden's file and should know he had only basic EVA combat training. Was this a joke?

"Yes, sir."

What else could he say? Pavlovich was probably still annoyed by his deploying the drones without orders, even though it was the obvious course of action. Was this a way to knock him down a few pegs—put him in his place?

It was a critical mission, far too important to screw around with. Certainly not a routine teaching opportunity suitable to humble a young officer who had overstepped his authority.

Perhaps it was something else. Maybe he intended to assess Hayden's leadership potential—justify his decision to make him XO? Why now? Was he willing risk the lives of the boarding party to satisfy his curiosity?

Pavlovich continued to appear amused. "You'll need to get fitted for a combat suit, Lieutenant. Gunney's boys are a lot bigger than you, so you may have to dig around to find one that fits."

The Rangers

TRUE TO THE CAPTAIN'S prediction, Hayden had difficulty finding an endo-skin that he didn't swim in. He settled on one designed for a woman that still hung loosely on his shoulders. Since it only had to provide a connection medium for the battle armour, he wasn't too concerned. Still, he thought it best to get it covered by the exo-layer before the Rangers arrived. They were a rough lot and would give him a hard time if they saw him struggling to put it on.

Built of seamlessly linked armoured panels, it weighed over a hundred kilograms before any weapons were attached. Fortunately, the weightless conditions made the job of dressing a simple one for him by himself.

With the two layers now covering him, his implant initiated the connection between the endo-skin and the outer battle layer. He flexed oversized, armoured hands and selected an arm cannon from the rack.

Now he wished the gravity was active. The combat suit was designed to augment his strength by over tenfold, and the weapon weighed in at over two hundred kilos. He wanted to enjoy effortlessly lifting it with one hand. As it was, he barely had time to attach it when the hatchway opened. He self-consciously floated away from the equipment rack to give the new arrivals all the room they needed.

Like Gunney, the Rangers tended to keep to themselves in their own dedicated section of the ship near the armoury.

It took a moment for him to realize that the first soldier that entered was a woman. Two metres tall, she outweighed him by at least fifteen kilos of muscle. A jagged scar ran from her right ear to the base of her lantern jaw. Her close-cropped dark hair revealed a tattoo of the Ranger coat of arms on her scalp. Her movements in the weightlessness were graceful for a woman of her size. She showed signs of augmentation. One eye was artificial, and her entire left arm, which at first appeared normal to him, had bare connector patches along it.

She was followed by a male, even larger than Gunney, if that was possible. Unlike the woman, his face was unmarked and handsome. He wore his hair longer, though the tracings of a similar tattoo could be made out in places beneath, and he showed no obvious cyborg enhancements.

Hayden was taken aback by the next two who entered the armoury. About the same size as the man, they were obviously synths. Their unremarkable faces were identical, and their inhuman eyes did not give him the impression of the intelligence he knew lay behind them.

Combat AIs were the norm, rather than the exception on most ships. Human Rangers, augmented or not, were rare and had not been regularly deployed by Earth Forces for the past fifteen years.

The woman floated closer to him. He stifled the urge to flinch as she saluted.

"Lieutenant Kaine, I am Chief Warrant Officer Atan."

She dutifully held the salute until Hayden realized she waited for him to return it. He raised his armour-encased right arm and tried not to strike his face. Before he could compose his response, she continued with the introductions.

"This is Corporal Enders," she indicated the man, then pointed to the synths, "and these are Ten-K-five, and One-K-two, though we call them Tin-key and Win-key." They saluted Hayden.

Self-conscious, he said, "Very good. Please carry on."

"Aye, sir."

She nodded to the others. They immediately moved to the racks and began donning their own combat gear.

"If I may, Lieutenant?"

"I'm sorry?"

She discreetly removed the cannon from his sleeve and turned it around to point in the opposite direction.

"Oh, I see. Um, thank you, Chief." His cheeks warmed.

Her smile was reassuring, despite her scars. "Don't worry, sir. Almost everyone does that at least once."

"I did it twice," said Enders from across the room.

She laughed. "That is true, he did."

She turned to rejoin her men. Hayden called her back. "Look, Chief. We both know how green I am. I may be the ranking officer in this little boarding party, but I'm just as likely to get everyone killed if left in charge..."

She nodded. "You want me to take command without letting the bridge think you aren't? I understand, sir. Your reputation is safe."

He protested that wasn't his intention when she continued.

"I want to thank you, Lieutenant."

"For what?"

"You recognized your limitations. Some officers would boldly assume command. That doesn't end well for them, or for my men."

He smiled. "You should get prepped, Chief."

She returned his smile. Somehow, she managed to pivot around in the zero gravity and drifted toward the equipment lockers.

He glanced over to where Enders minded his own business, adjusting a fitting on his helmet. The two synths also ignored him.

Even though he was still in zero-G, the armour and weapons seemed a great deal lighter.

Discovery

THE BOARDING PARTY stood before *Scimitar's* airlock, their magnetic boots holding them securely in place. Hayden was connected with every member of the squad and the tactical station on the bridge through his helmet's HUD.

At his signal, the hatch was opened to the connection causeway between *Scimitar* and the other ship. Tin-key and Enders released their mag locks and floated down the tunnel to the closed airlock at the other end. After a minute, they signalled the all-clear, and the rest of the team followed.

By the time Hayden and the others arrived, the outer doorway to the wreck was open. Enders and Tin-key awaited them inside.

"It looks like gravity plating is active over here, sir!" said Atan.

Despite her warning, he was unprepared for the abrupt transition. He struggled to maintain his poise as he settled to the deck and wondered how foolish he appeared.

Seeking to distract from his awkward entrance, he said, "Did you get that, *Scimitar*? Gravity is functioning."

"Acknowledged," replied Pavlovich. "Proceed as planned. Exercise extreme caution. Oh, and Kaine?"

"Yes, sir?"

"If you are smart, you'll let Atan take control of the situation from here."

Hayden smiled. He had just been tossed a lifeline for his reputation with the crew. Had that been the test? Did the captain anticipate how big a mess of things he would make all by himself?

"That is a very good suggestion, sir. I believe I shall do that very thing." He heard Pavlovich exhale with relief.

"Chief Atan, as per the captain's order, I defer to your good judgement. Please assume command."

"Aye-aye, Lieutenant."

Hayden couldn't see her face through her tinted visor, but he assumed she wore a knowing smile.

She closed the outer door, automatically initiating the airlock's compression cycle.

At least the ship's systems are operational, thought Hayden.

After one final check that her team was in position, Atan said, "Sir, it is probably best if you hang back and allow my men to ensure the ship is safe to enter."

He nodded and moved behind the squad. When everyone was ready, she activated the doorway mechanism, and the hatch swung open.

One by one, weapons raised, the team advanced through the opening, leaving Hayden alone. After an anxious minute, his headset crackled with Atan's voice.

"All is secured, sir. We've found something you need to see."

He stepped into the interior of the old warship. The few lighting panels in the walls that were active flickered intermittently and shone on stirred up dust, making it sparkle. Despite the internal cooling of his suit, he sweated profusely.

Thirty metres down the hallway, two of the Rangers had their guns trained on something. As he moved closer, he saw they had their weapons pointed at a frightened middle-aged man and a young woman. They were both on their knees in the dust, hands clasped behind their heads.

Hayden's implant kicked out an image from the ship's database that identified the older man.

He was none other than Doctor Ishmael Gabriel, the missing scientist.

Ishmael Gabriel

THE MAN AND WOMAN WERE brought aboard *Scimitar* and placed in isolation. Over the following twenty-two hours, the medical synths poked, prodded, and took samples until the pair was cleared of carrying pathogens. They suffered from nothing more serious than malnutrition. Genetic tests confirmed the man to be Ishmael Gabriel, and the woman, while not in the database, tested as his daughter.

When Hayden caught up with them in medical, they were wolfing down a meal and appeared more energetic than when he first encountered them.

"Doctor, I am Lieutenant Kaine, first officer of the *Scimitar*. The captain sends his regrets and asked me to debrief you." He had no idea what commanded Pavlovich's attention and wondered if this was another kind of test.

"Yes, yes, of course," said Gabriel around a mouthful of food. He was short and rail thin. His scraggly black beard was peppered with ample amounts of white, and his long, greying hair was tied into a neat bun. He invited Hayden to sit across from them.

The scientist wiped his mouth and then directed Hayden's attention to the young woman. She appeared to be in her late teens, small-framed and thin. Her unkempt, mousy brown hair fell over her eyes, which regarded him with suspicion.

"This is my daughter, Stella."

"It is nice to meet you," said Hayden, extending his hand to her. She stared at him for a moment then returned to her food tray.

"Please forgive her, Lieutenant. She hasn't met many people in her twenty years, and I'm afraid I was lax in teaching her the social graces."

"She's lived out here her entire life?"

"She was born out here. Her mother died when Stella was an infant, and I raised her myself."

"Neither of you had any other human contact in all that time?"

"I didn't say that. We've had occasional encounters with some of the other survivors."

"How many are there, and where are they?"

"Not as many as there once were. A few hundred, maybe? My wife and I were trapped here when the light-gate went offline."

Hayden swallowed, recalling his own anxiety when *Scimitar* lost contact with it.

"We are scattered through the system, scraping together a nomadic existence with whatever resources can be salvaged. We all stay on the move to evade the Malliac patrols."

"The what?"

"Oh, that is what I named them. They are the race who destroyed Dulcinea."

"They are still around? How did you avoid them?"

Gabriel laughed, and Stella smiled, sharing a private joke.

"Space, even in a planetary system, is big, Lieutenant. Was it pure luck that we avoided them? I don't know for sure. They rarely return to a location they've searched, as far as I can tell."

"What are they searching for?"

Gabriel shrugged. "Alas, I do not know. When they encounter a ship, they disable it and rip it apart, killing anyone they find. We've learned to watch for any sign of their approach and take actions to hide."

"What kind of signs? Do they possess stealth technology?" Hayden's thoughts were drawn to their own attacker.

Gabriel's eyes stared off into space while he considered the question. "I doubt they think of themselves as having such."

"You'll have to explain that to me, Doctor."

"To the best of my knowledge, based on my study of the Glenatat ruins on Dulcinea, the Malliac are not like us. They come from regions of the galaxy composed of dark matter."

Hayden tried to recall his physics classes. If their ships were built of the stuff, it explained why only the rail gun had any effect on them.

"How is it you came to be here, Lieutenant? Is the light-gate active again?"

"It was but has stopped talking to us since our arrival. Do you know anything about that?"

Gabriel shook his head. "Believe me, if I knew why it isn't working, most of my time would be spent trying to locate and repair it. It seems to function well enough to guide ships across to this side, as evidenced by your presence, but once here, they become trapped like flies on fly paper."

"I beg your pardon. I don't understand what you mean."

"Sorry. I'm a historian and archaeologist. It's a reference to an obscure nineteenth century technology for catching insect pests."

Stella seemed amused by Hayden's confusion.

"So, you think these Malliac wait near the light-gate to waylay any ships that enter the system?"

Gabriel nodded and after a moment's consideration spoke around a mouthful of half-chewed food. "Mmmm...that is one theory. But based on their wider-ranging activity, I think they may be looking for something. We just give them a wide berth."

"Why were you aboard the wreck of the UEF *Odyssey*?"

"Well, to hide, but I thought it a wonderful opportunity to study the history of a ship from that era."

"There was life support in the section we found you in. Was it active when you boarded?"

Gabriel's laughter filled the room. "Oh, no, Lieutenant, most certainly not. We got the environmental system running again. Stella is adept at engineering solutions."

Hayden regarded the famished pixie who continued to stuff herself with food.

"How long had you been there?"

"I tend to lose track of time. I think about ten months, give or take?"

"And where were you before?"

"Oh, pretty much everywhere. We've spent time in the asteroid mines and on some of the abandoned research stations on the outer planets. We even lived for two years on the surface of Dulcinea. We would have stayed longer, but our CO_2 scrubbers failed and we were forced to beat a hasty escape."

"What were you doing on the planet?"

"Why, studying the Glenatat ruins, of course. I needed to verify some of my theories by examining the actual site, or what was left of it. One can only learn so much from 3D holo-recordings, you know. I sent all my conclusions in my last two reports. When I didn't get any response, I was forced to assume the worst."

"They were received, Doctor. How long ago did you send them?"

"Um, well, fifteen or sixteen years, I believe. The light-gate was not accepting transmissions, so I placed them in a courier drone and sent them to the gate at Hip-85."

"What did you mean when you said you'd assumed the worst?"

"I thought the Earth had been destroyed."

"By what?"

He sighed, as if dealing with a slow student. "You didn't read my reports?"

Hayden shook his head. What Iris had showed him was only a redacted summary, but based on what he now heard, he was convinced that this was the unknown author of that document.

"Unbelievable." Gabriel threw his bread crust to the plate. "Why are you here?"

"We were sent to recover you and return you to Earth. Why do you think we are here?"

"I thought you came to follow up about Glenatat star-gate technology."

"You mean to tell me they possessed FTL capability?"

Gabriel straightened in his seat, indignant. "They most certainly did. They were an elder race. Did no one read—" He sighed and tried to calm down. "As I explained in my reports that nobody read: to reach their home world. They are the only ones with the ability to stop the Malliac, as they did twenty-five thousand years ago. They are the only chance to save the Earth and every inhabited star system."

Making a Run

THE CAPTAIN'S QUARTERS were only marginally larger than Hayden's own, yet he insisted on holding meetings there. Hayden, Cora, and Ishmael Gabriel sat crammed around a small desk in the middle of the room while the captain used his bunk as a chair.

"Let's go over it all again," said Pavlovich. "Engineering report?"

"Repairs are mostly completed, Cap'n. I scrounged some surplus gravity plating, hull armour, and circuitry and put it to good use. Turns out *Odyssey* and *Scimitar* are of similar age and share a lot of common tech." Cora was chipper and spoke rapidly, as Hayden had learned was normal when she was excited.

"Weapons?"

"*Odyssey's* armoury was in a separate section of the wreckage," said Kaine. "We located it, but it was mostly depleted. Gunney brought whatever he thought useful aboard."

"So they put up a fight?"

"A substantial one, it seems. We found the aft piece, and its laser generators were burned out. The rail guns were operational but had no ammo."

"What about the fore section?"

"Nothing left of it. It was likely destroyed before the rest of the ship broke apart."

Pavlovich eyed Hayden before he spoke. "*Odyssey* was a class-one dreadnought. It would take an incredible amount of firepower to do that much damage."

"I recommend we execute repairs and find a way out of the system as fast as possible, sir. We don't stand a chance if they find us. I think we caught our pursuer by surprise, but I doubt we'll be as lucky again if they return."

The small room was warm with so many bodies in it, and perspiration trickled down Hayden's neck.

Pavlovich spoke to the scientist. "You mentioned that the Malliac are searching for something. Care to speculate as to what?"

Gabriel stared thoughtfully at the captain. "I can't say for sure, but the engineering section of any ship we've found has been torn apart."

"How about it, Cora? What did you find on *Odyssey*?"

"A huge mess, Cap'n. The damage was not from the attack itself. The light-gate engines were ripped to shreds."

Hayden asked, "Any chance the aliens were trying to see how it worked?"

She smiled, like he'd said something cute. "If they did, they had a real odd way about it. Components weren't disassembled. They were destroyed."

"What about the energy chamber for the jump drive?

"It was in the same condition as the rest of engineering, Cap'n."

"What happened to the microsingularity?"

"That is the strange part. It was gone. My guess is that the Malliac took it."

"Maybe they're trapped here too and need one to leave?" said Hayden.

"Maybe..." said Pavlovich. "Doctor, you mentioned these aliens are from regions of dark matter?"

"Yes. Records I've studied refer to them as the invisible ones."

"If that is true, they would be undetectable by our instruments," said Kaine.

The captain nodded at him then probed Gabriel further. "Does your research tell you how the Glenatat defeated them?"

"The ruins were badly damaged even before our colony was established. All I know is that they were victorious, but there are only fragmentary references as to how."

"Hmm, so much for that idea," said Hayden. "That brings us back to our own malfunctioning light-gate."

Pavlovich frowned. "Options?"

"We don't have the equipment to repair it if it is damaged, Cap'n," Cora said.

"Even if did, we would be vulnerable while we hung around to fix it. For the moment, assume we've lost our ticket home. Other ideas?"

"Well, the next obvious answer is to kick in the star drive and make a run to the nearest colony with an active jump-gate," said Hayden.

"Which would only take fifteen years at our top-rated speed," said Pavlovich. "We wouldn't age much, and if the good doctor is correct, there might not be a home by the time we arrive."

"There is the Glenatat star-gate, Captain," said Gabriel.

"Tell me about this thing."

"Well, it was in my reports, but since nobody has bothered..." He caught the icy stares of Pavlovich and Kaine.

"Ah, yes, well...things being as they are, I will explain. According to the records I found, both are elder races, meaning they were advanced civilizations long before humanity dug ourselves out of the last ice age. They fought each other in a galactic-scale conflict."

"That is an interesting history lesson. Is there a point to it?"

"Yes, Captain. The Malliac were defeated because they did not possess the same means to traverse great distances as their enemy. They are relegated to travelling at sub-light speeds; the Glenatat were not. I happen to know where the star-gate in the system is located."

"What good does their technology do us?" said Hayden. "We don't have the knowledge to access it."

Gabriel glowered at him. "I did not claim I knew all the answers, Lieutenant. I merely share what I learned."

"Do your records tell you what this star-gate is? How it functions?"

"It is stable, Captain. I suppose the only description of it we would understand is to call it a wormhole, but that is imprecise."

"Where does it go?" asked Hayden.

"They operated a network of these gates throughout their empire. I only mapped out a fraction of it, but all of them lead to their home world..."

"Which helps us how?"

"You need to understand that while Earth's FTL system is extensive, comprising now over a hundred star systems, the Glenatat version serviced a vast dominion of over a million planets. I would be greatly shocked if there are no other gates that access some of the same stars we do, just as they did here at Mu Arae."

Hayden began to reply, but Pavlovich put a hand on his arm to stop him and addressed the scientist. "So, do you suggest we find it to travel to their planet and ask for directions and a means to defeat the Malliac?"

"Well, that is rather simplistic, but yes."

The captain considered him for several long seconds. "Doctor, please supply your coordinates for this thing to Mister Kaine. If it happens to lie near where we are going, it might be worth the time to look for it."

"Where are we going, Cap'n?" asked Cora.

"There is no practical choice. We will make our way to the closest Confederation outpost with a light-gate. Everyone should pack a lunch. This is going to be a long road trip."

Stella

ALONE IN HIS OWN CRAMPED quarters, Hayden paced the small floor space and attempted to make sense of what happened.

The meeting had ended with Pavlovich ordering completion of repairs and a course plotted to the location of the alien wormhole. By some massive coincidence, it lay on a slight deviation from the most direct route to the closest active light-gate.

The captain was more desperate than he let on. That was the only explanation Hayden could come up with for his entertainment of Gabriel's insane idea. At least travelling at relativistic speeds to the nearest occupied system had a predictable outcome. If they located the doctor's star-gate and discovered a way to access it, where would it take them?

Who was this guy anyway? Why was he so important that a military ship needed to be sent to rescue him? More importantly, why had Hayden been chosen for this mission?

There were a hundred undesirable assignments the Old Man could select from as a suitable sanction for him to endure. Why did he pick this one? The *Scimitar* was held together by scrounged parts and a creative miracle worker who wasn't even an official engineer. The commanding officer was some washout nearing retirement and had been put out here to keep him out of the admiral's hair. Hayden wondered if that was his own intended fate.

Assuming he didn't die or screw up and wind up in the brig like his predecessor; assuming he decided to embrace the idea of a life in the military over a diplomatic one, and managed some degree of advancement; assuming they could find a way out of this godforsaken system on the edge of known space—was Hayden's fate to be that of Pavlovich? An undistinguished career spent on an insignificant ship exiled to the farthest reaches of human habitation.

He threw himself on his bunk and covered his face with his pillow. It smelled of someone else's shampoo and vaguely like vomit. Disgusted, he hurled it across the room, where it landed on his bag. He realized he had not unpacked yet and wondered what that said about his acceptance of his situation.

He wanted to go home.

He missed his old apartment that he hardly ever slept in, and Kyle's nagging micromanagement of his life. He regretted no longer being a cadet officer whose only real responsibility was passing enough courses to graduate and not upset his father in the process.

All his life, he was able to sweet-talk his way out of situations his antics landed him in. What persuasion couldn't accomplish, Dad's influence could. His life had always worked out for him that way; at least until recently.

It was a rude awakening to discover the low esteem the admiral held his father in. Maybe, just to spite his father, the Old Man had picked this assignment to make a point. Or points.

The first was that he was expected to find advancement on his own merit. It was clear that the only way back to the career path he wanted was to rely on his own abilities and not fall back on luck or privilege. He had to earn his way out of this situation and demonstrate that he deserved to be back on Earth, where the action was. He would be required to do something spectacular to accomplish that. Maybe contacting an alien race and helping save humanity would be just the ticket?

The admiral's other message was more personal. Hayden had gone too far and broken Katie's heart. Her grandfather took that personally. He might have to wait until the Old Man died before he ever found his way home. He'd really screwed up and had no way to even begin to fix it.

The memories of Katie poured forth in an overwhelming flood. He missed the warmth of her body next to his; the subtle scent of her favourite soap. Her strength of character, her amazing intellect, her unrelenting dedication to her work, her sense of humour, her patient and forgiving nature.

He'd managed to hold back the recollections and the regrets since that day in front of her office. The journey to *Scimitar* and the rapid flow of events had kept his mind occupied until physical exhaustion forced him into dreamless sleep. The last thing he needed, he now realized, was down time to indulge in self-pity.

He sat up and wiped the wetness from his cheeks. Perhaps Kwok required some assistance in locating the wormhole. If not, he was sure Cora could put him to work.

The buzzer to his door sounded. The crew always flagged him on his implant if they needed him. He stared stupidly at the closed door, wondering who would pay him a visit like this.

It buzzed a second time. He walked to the door and after only a second's hesitation opened it to Stella. Her eyes were moist, and she appeared disturbed about something.

"Stella? What can I do for you?"

Determination crossed her face, and she placed her hand on his chest, pushing him back into his quarters with far more strength than her size belied. The door closed behind her, and she looked about the room, confusion clouding her face.

"Is something wrong?"

Her gaze fixed on him, and the look of determination returned. Without any warning, she lunged at him, throwing her arms around his neck. She pressed her lips to his with such force that it hurt. Inertia carried them both to his bunk, where she fell on top of him, never breaking her lip lock.

She covered his face with rapid, desperate kisses and ground her supple young body to his. Her knee pushed aggressively into his groin. She grabbed his right hand and pressed it to her small breast.

When the shock of her amorous assault passed, he found himself submitting to the moment, returning her kisses, trying to slow down the pace to a more sensual one. She responded to his cues and wriggled sensuously against him.

Realizing how inappropriate his behaviour was, he opened his eyes and gently but firmly disengaged from her embrace.

"Please, stop. We can't do this." He couldn't believe what he heard himself saying. Spontaneous trysts were not an unusual occurrence for him. Even while he dated Katie, he had succumbed to similar temptations, but usually when both parties were under the influence of alcohol. It was against his character to dissuade willing women from going to bed with him, but something about Stella was off. He couldn't explain it, but there was something about the situation that suggested she did not realize what she was doing.

She struggled for a few seconds to reinitiate their coupling then abruptly sat on the edge of the bed and gazed into space. Hayden leapt off the bunk and stared at her, but she did not look at him.

"I don't want to hurt your feelings. You are a very attractive woman, but..."

"I felt your pain." Her voice was faint, and she continued to stare blankly ahead.

"I'm sorry?"

She looked at him, tears running down her cheeks. "I shared your sadness. I thought I could help you make it all go away."

He didn't know how to respond. The girl was crazier than her old man.

He helped her to her feet. "Why don't we pay a visit to the infirmary? Do you know where your father is?"

She shook her head and allowed him to escort her out of his quarters. He was grateful that nobody was in the hallway to see them exit.

When they were halfway to the medical centre, Stella's back stiffened and her limbs went rigid. Terror contorted her features, and her mouth opened and closed, uttering silent words.

Her hands flew to her head, and she dropped to her knees. The mournful scream of a banshee erupted from her, and she rocked back and forth, pulling her hair from her head. He stood, helpless in front of her.

Two crewmen rushed down the corridor to investigate the source of the commotion. At the sight of them, Hayden snapped into action and issued orders. One assisted him to carry the screaming girl into the infirmary while the other went to locate Doctor Gabriel and the captain.

By the time the medical synths had strapped Stella to a bed, her father rushed through the doorway and to the side of his pitiful daughter. She seized his hand and squeezed her nails into his flesh until she drew blood. He endured it without comment, like it was a common occurrence.

"What the hell is wrong with her, Doctor?"

He ignored Hayden and fought to gain Stella's attention. "Stella! Tell me what it is."

He feared that she would begin confessing the events in his quarters and accuse him of assaulting her. She shook her head and struggled against the restraints. One of the synths approached with a hypo. Gabriel stopped him.

"No, not yet!" He grasped her head and forced her to look him in the eyes. "Stella! It's Papa. What did you see?"

She halted her struggle and locked her gaze on his, though terror still filled her eyes.

Her voice croaked. "Them."

"You're sure? "

She nodded, and tears flowed. Gabriel fought back his own and caressed her cheek. He turned to the medical synth holding the hypospray and indicated he should proceed. He didn't step away from the bed until the sedative was administered and the girl began to drift off to sleep.

"What the hell was that all about, Doctor?" said Pavlovich, who had entered unnoticed during the commotion.

Ishmael Gabriel regarded both him and Hayden. "Captain, we are in grave danger. The Malliac are on their way here."

Pavlovich's brow furrowed, and his face reddened. "I thought you said they don't revisit sites they already searched?"

"No...no, I said they don't usually return, except when...unless they make a connection."

Confused, Hayden and Pavlovich stared at each other, then both regarded the distracted scientist. After a few seconds, an explanation burst forth from him.

"Stella is an empath. She can experience the emotions of others, sometimes without being aware of it. It is the reason why we avoided contact with other people for most of her life. It is so difficult for everyone."

"I think I know something about that," said Hayden, "but what has that to do with the Malliac?"

"We discovered very early that Stella forms a strong connection to them when they are near. At first it was a vague premonition that she gave voice to. We learned quickly to trust her premonitions and to hide or move on before they arrived. But later, after several such encounters, her experiences became more intense—more visceral. I think the aliens can determine our location through Stella's empathic abilities."

"Can they detect her when she is sedated like this?" asked the Captain.

Gabriel looked at his sleeping daughter and touched her hand. "No. When she first senses them, I administer a sedative before the connection becomes too strong."

"She experienced an intense reaction," said Hayden.

"I have been administering a mild calmative drug to her since you found us. For the longest time it has been only the two of us. With so many people aboard this ship...perhaps she was tempted by all the emotions around her and went off the meds. If she did that, the strength and abundance of the crew's feelings would overwhelm the subtle first signs of contact. She possibly didn't notice the Malliac probing for her."

Hayden watched the sleeping girl and felt a wave of guilt.

"So, there is a reasonable chance that they won't sniff around if they lost their connection?" said Pavlovich.

"I'm afraid not, Captain. Her response was very strong; the strongest in many years. I suspect they have a very good idea of where to look."

"Well, crap!" He stalked across the room and accessed an interface on the wall. "Bridge! Sound battle stations. Prepare for departure in..." He looked questioningly at Gabriel.

"Perhaps twenty minutes before they arrive, but it may be sooner," said the doctor.

"Double shit!" Pavlovich pressed the button again and spoke to the comm link again. "Make ready to depart immediately. Cora, send out the bugs again to see if we can pick up their static." He terminated the connection before anyone could respond.

"It would have been nice to know about this when we picked you up, Doctor." He turned on his heel and stormed out of the infirmary.

Hayden looked at Stella. How she must have suffered being around so many people she didn't know and not being allowed to experience her gift. He imagined the proximity of the crew was too tempting for her to resist. He knew from his own life how overwhelming temptation could be.

He'd never met an empath before and had only heard second-hand stories about them. As far as he knew, most of them were institutionalized in their early teens. Those who didn't get locked up and regularly sedated often committed suicide or found their way to isolated places with few people around to mess them up.

As he began to leave, Gabriel called to his back.

"Lieutenant, there may be something I can do to help."

"What is it, Doctor?"

"One of the tactics we've used in the past has been to offer the Malliac a distraction to allow our escape. We employ it far earlier, but it still might work."

Impatient, Hayden asked, "What do you have in mind?"

"Drones. I have several specialized ones on my ship, which is stored in your hangar. When we detect an event, I launch one to distract the aliens so we can slip away."

"Were you responsible for the probe that met us at the light gate?"

"Yes, most certainly, though I don't understand why you had to destroy it."

"What is on your drone that grabs the aliens' interest?"

The scientist blushed and hesitated before he answered. "I'm afraid the Malliac are not the only ones who were hunting for microsingularities. I, too, have been harvesting them from wrecked star drives in this system. I install them in my probes and send them out. They serve as an excellent bait."

"So, you give them what they are looking for?"

"I suppose so, but you would do the same to survive."

"There is no need to be defensive, Doctor. I can't fault your motivation. And you're right. I would likely do something similar were I in your situation. How soon can you launch a drone?"

"I can deploy one within a couple of minutes."

"Okay, proceed. I'll inform the captain."

Hayden took a final glance at the peaceful face of Stella. He advised Pavlovich of the plan over the comm and then left orders with the medical synth to keep the girl under until further notice. As he walked to the bridge, he hoped his faith in Gabriel was not misplaced and that *Scimitar* could slip away unnoticed.

There was no way they could survive another battle.

Stella Sedated

SCIMITAR had been underway for seventy-three days without incident. The tension aboard the ship since their hasty escape from the wreck of the *Odyssey* had been eroded down to boredom by routine.

Doctor Gabriel's tactic of baiting the Malliac with a drone proved effective, though it had taken several weeks of travel at one-quarter light speed to convince the captain they had shaken their ghostly pursuer.

Using the coordinates supplied by the scientist, the *Scimitar* exited the Mu Arae system in search of the mysterious alien star-gate. The fact that most of the crew didn't believe the wormhole existed was immaterial; unable to access their own light-gate and pursued by hostiles, there was little other choice than to attempt to find Gabriel's unicorn or face more than a decade of space travel.

Hayden was uneasy not having the use of the orbital bugs, but they were not capable of operating at relativistic speeds, despite Cora's best efforts to address the limitation. They had spent the first ten days travelling at slower velocity, carefully monitoring their wake for any sign of the static discharge. When nothing appeared over that time, Pavlovich ordered the drones retrieved and their speed increased.

Hayden rubbed his temples, grateful that the headaches were finished. They had become increasingly intense over the past couple of weeks, and at the captain's order, he had been forced to endure a complete physical workup. Pavlovich seemed to worry that the empathic encounter with the girl might be the cause. It turned out to be a fault in his implant.

It was rare for the LINK tech to fail, but it did happen. There was no way to repair the damage with the resources aboard. More sophisticated facilities on Earth were needed for that. The medical synth told him the headaches would go away as he became accustomed to no longer having an implant.

For the first time since his arrival, he was grateful to be assigned to the outdated vessel. Without his LINK, his role as XO on a more modern warship would be hopeless to fulfill. As things stood, he could still perform the bulk of his duties using the ship's antique manual interfaces, though he found himself exhausted from the unfamiliar effort. Pavlovich, while somewhat sympathetic to his new disadvantage, did not cut him much slack in what was expected.

As was his habit at the end of his shift, he went to the infirmary to check on Stella. She had been kept under heavy sedation since their departure from Mu Arae, and he felt responsible for her current fate.

The lights in her room were dimmed, and only the blinking face of the medical equipment gave any illumination. Hayden, as he did every time, stood at the side of the bed and held her hand. He didn't know if she was aware of him, but he wanted to try to assure her on some level that she was not forgotten.

A movement in the corner of the room startled him.

"I think she would like that you come to see her," said Cora from the shadows. She reclined in a chair and looked like she had just woken up.

"I wouldn't know about that. I just think of it as something I would appreciate if I were in her place."

"You're a nice man, Lieutenant."

Hayden was grateful the dim light hid his warming cheeks. "You wouldn't say that if you knew me better, Cora."

"I dunno. Travelling together in this flying can reveals a person's character. It's hard to not get real." He sensed her smiling in the darkness.

"Do you visit often?" he asked.

"I come when I can. I think I was more tired than I thought last night, because I fell asleep in this chair. This is one of the most peaceful places on the ship. You can barely hear the hums, pings, and pops of the hull."

"I suppose even you might need a break from *Scimitar* on occasion."

"Oh, I don't need any real breaks except to sleep. I love this old boat. She takes a lot of work, and keeping her flying is more than a full-time job, but there is something special about her that makes it less like a labour. Do you know what I mean?"

"I don't think I've been aboard long enough to appreciate that."

"And somebody's waiting for you back home, isn't she?"

His heart ached as he realized how far he was from Katie in more ways than one.

Cora stood and stretched before walking to the opposite side of Stella's bed. The blue lights of the equipment lit her face like a kabuki actor's. She reached across the bed and put her hand on top of his. "Time and distance can heal, Lieutenant."

She looked down at Stella's peaceful face and adjusted a wayward strand of hair on her forehead. "If she were awake, she could probably tell you what you are really feeling. It is quite a gift this girl has. I hope the cap'n lets her wake up soon to enjoy it."

She looked into Hayden's eyes and added, "So that we all can benefit from it."

Cora strode leisurely to the doorway and spoke to him without turning around. "Goodnight, Lieutenant."

With her gone, the room fell into a silence periodically broken by the clicks of the devices connected to Stella.

Hayden wondered if she dreamed while she was under. A flash of resentment rose up in him on her behalf. It wasn't right for Pavlovich to keep her sedated. Her father had argued for her to be allowed to awaken and be managed with a mild sedative, but the captain feared she would prove to be a beacon in the darkness for the Malliac.

Stella's eyebrow twitched and turned to a slight frown. Had she heard, or rather, felt Hayden's emotions on the matter? He released her hand and stepped back from the bed.

Perhaps it was his proximity, or even the physical contact with her that allowed her to connect to him, even under sedation.

If that was even what had happened.

Maybe it was just a dream she experienced. But the timing of it was too coincidental for him to easily accept that argument.

Maybe Pavlovich was right. It might be better off for everyone if she remained asleep.

Pavlovich Relents

"PLEASE, CAPTAIN?"

Ishmael Gabriel was nearly in tears.

"I will tell what I told you two days ago, Doctor. Your daughter will remain sedated." The captain glared at the scientist to emphasize his point and then returned his attention to his cooling supper.

The distraught father turned to Hayden, who had followed him into the captain's quarters. "Lieutenant, can't you reason with this man?"

Pavlovich fixed his first officer with a withering look. Kaine frowned, annoyed he was caught between the two men on this issue.

"He has a valid argument, Captain. We've been accelerating toward maximum sub-light for the past few weeks. We can't use the drones to check our flank. If we want any kind of warning we are being followed, the young woman's abilities are the only available option...unless we choose to reduce velocity and deploy the bugs."

"We might as well stop dead in our tracks if we do that," the captain said, directing his sarcasm at Gabriel, "since we don't know where we are going or what we are looking for."

"I told you that we search for..."

"All I received from you is a set of coordinates that you assure me is the location of the wormhole. We will reach that destination in six hours, and so far there is no indication of anything ahead of us."

"There is some degree of uncertainty to be expected in translating such things into our units of measurement. We may be off by a small amount, but I assure you it is there." A sheen of sweat glistened on Gabriel's forehead.

"What do you consider an acceptable margin for error? An AU? Half a parsec? Two?"

"No, nothing that large..."

"I'll be frank with you, Doctor. I never believed in your fairy tale about an ancient race or a wormhole. The only reason I indulged you was because the coordinates you gave were only a slight deviation from a direct course to a system with an active light-gate. We will lose, at most, a few weeks by looking, and I can tell my commanding officer that we did not ignore you, thereby covering my own ass when we eventually return you to Earth. Not that it will matter, as everyone I answer to will be long retired or dead."

He turned his attention to Hayden. "Mister Kaine, I believe we have spent far too much time on this snipe hunt. Give orders to adjust our heading to GI613 and increase our acceleration to maximum."

"Captain, no!" pleaded Gabriel.

Hayden felt pity for the man, whose entire life's work was at the point of being either confirmed or refuted. However, he was inclined to be of a similar mind as Pavlovich. They couldn't afford the fuel or the time to stop to look for something that might not exist.

"Sir, with respect, I checked the computations, and we can hold our current velocity at point three-six C for twelve more hours before we lose our trajectory window. May I recommend that we devote a little more time to the search? As a precaution against pursuit, we can awaken the girl."

"Is there any guarantee that she can detect these aliens while traveling at relativistic speeds?"

"I...I don't know," said Gabriel.

"I thought not," said Pavlovich. His expression softened, and he continued, "But we are flying blind, and it would be nice to know if they are following us."

Gabriel's eyes brightened. "I can keep her sedated. I am familiar with the appropriate dosage. She stopped taking them without my knowledge when we came aboard. I can make sure that doesn't happen again."

"Will it affect her sensitivity to the Malliac?" asked Hayden.

"Only slightly."

Pavlovich put down his fork and stared at the anxious Gabriel for several long seconds. He shook his head. "Very well, it isn't healthy for her to be kept under, so I grant you permission to awaken her. Mister Kaine, we will proceed with your plan, but I am making you personally responsible for the girl. If she shows the slightest indication of contact with the aliens, she is to be put back to sleep immediately. Am I understood?"

"Yes, sir, I understand," replied Hayden.

"Thank you so very much, Captain. You will not regret this," said Gabriel.

"I already do, Doctor. We will spend the next twelve hours looking for your wormhole, but not a second longer. Now will you two please leave so I can finish my supper in peace?"

"I'm fine, Lieutenant Kaine. Just a little weak from lying in a bed for so long. I appreciate you showing me around the ship. The walking is good exercise for me."

Hayden and Stella strolled slowly along a corridor of the engineering section. Her demeanour toward him was shy. Perhaps she was ashamed of their last encounter in his quarters. They hadn't spoken much of that event, since neither of them seemed particularly comfortable with the topic.

Sometimes, when he recalled it, Hayden found himself amused and even a bit proud. He liked to imagine that his animal magnetism was what originally drew Stella to throw herself at him. But at other times, when his ego didn't run so hot, he was embarrassed for the poor girl who was driven by forces beyond her ability to moderate.

She was like a leaf on the wind. Her entire life was spent isolated from anyone other than her father. She must have experienced the chaotic emotional mélange of so many crewmen like a small boat on a stormy sea. She didn't come to him because of any natural attraction; she was drawn to his doorstep by the strength of the emotions he had put out.

The mild sedative seemed to be working, though Hayden was also conscious of his emotional state and tried to remain professionally detached while around her. She seemed so small and vulnerable, and he didn't want to be responsible for anything that might overpower the drug and send her back to the infirmary.

He deliberately selected more isolated sections of the ship for this tour, as far from the crew quarters and common areas as possible. Down here, Cora's engineering team were the only ones they were likely to encounter, and they were too busy on their work. Besides, Cora had a gentle spirit that Hayden didn't worry would stimulate Stella's empathic abilities.

They stopped in front of one of the few external viewports. The stars hung still in the distance.

"It is hard to believe we are moving," she said, mirroring his thoughts.

He looked at her askance and wondered for a moment if she was also telepathic.

He pointed at a random star and said, "If we were to watch carefully, we would see parallax shifts, but their movements are very slow..."

"Because they are so far away, and we aren't moving close enough to the speed of light yet," she said, completing his sentence. "My entire life has been spent in one spaceship or another, Lieutenant."

Hayden said, "Of course. I'm sorry for being condescending."

She smiled at him and returned her eyes to the window. "Actually, you were kind of cute."

"Your father paid attention to your education," he said, hoping a neutral topic would distract him from his feelings. He wondered if they flashed before Stella like a red cape in front of a bull. He didn't like the prospect of being so exposed.

"I am educated to the equivalent of two doctorates in archaeology and astronomy."

"How old are you?"

"Twenty," she said while she stared out the view port, an amused half smile on her face.

Hayden shook his head. Why was he always drawn to the brilliant ones?

His pulse accelerated when he realized what he just asked himself. Was he attracted to Stella? They only met a few weeks ago and had only one significant, if intense and ill-fated encounter.

He jumped, slightly, as she slipped her hand slip into his. His heart pounded, and he didn't know if it was from fear or excitement. He looked at her, and she returned his gaze. Whose emotions was he experiencing? Were they his own, or was she broadcasting her feelings to him?

He disentangled his fingers from her grip. "Stella, we really shouldn't..."

She took a step back and raised her hands to her temples. "Yes, of course you're right. We should keep our emotions neutral."

She grimaced and doubled over in pain.

"What's wrong?"

"I don't know...oh! It feels like burning needles."

She looked up, the same expression of horror on her face as before. "It's them..." She pitched forward, falling into Hayden's arms.

A flash of intense, unfamiliar, and alien emotions washed over Hayden. The experience was almost debilitating as he held Stella's now limp body. Vivid images burst upon his consciousness. A bizarre ship designed to look more like a beetle with a hundred legs and antennae jutting out at all angles. It glowed an eerie fluorescent blue. Views of *Scimitar* and feelings that reminded him of Stella filled his awareness.

Hayden instinctively tried to flag the bridge with his deactivated LINK. He cursed under his breath and picked her up. He called out for help, but nobody responded.

He rounded the corner and almost tripped over a body on the floor. Putting Stella down, he bent over the inert form of Cora and felt for a pulse. She was alive.

He looked farther up the corridor to see two other crewmen, lying motionless. Panic seized his guts as he lifted Stella and ran toward the infirmary. Every crewman he passed was either unconscious or rolling on the deck, clutching their head in pain.

He burst into the medical centre, grateful to see the synths were unaffected. They took charge of the young woman, administering the same sedatives they'd administered before.

"How many others are affected?" he asked.

"We are getting multiple alerts throughout the engineering and science sections of the ship," it said.

Those were the areas he had carried Stella through. Maybe whatever happened to them was limited to her proximity. He was positive that she must be the cause of the incapacitation of the crew.

Hayden moved to the wall console and activated a voice link to the bridge. "This is Kaine. Crewmen down in section D. Is anyone affected up there?"

Pavlovich's angry voice responded through the speakers. "Several people got sudden headaches, but nobody is down. What the hell is going on? Is the girl responsible?"

"I honestly don't know, sir. I think so; she's in medical now and the synths are putting her under again. But there is a bigger problem. The Malliac found us and are on their way."

The Malliac

HAYDEN BURST THROUGH the hatchway, breathless. He quickly assessed the situation on the bridge. All the crew were focused on their tasks, in no apparent distress.

"Is everyone all right?" he asked as he assumed his station.

"A nagging hangnail still bothers me, and my stools are a little loose lately, but otherwise, I'm fine. How are you, Lieutenant? Nice of you to join us." Hayden still was not used to the captain's sense of humour.

"I mean, is anyone still affected by...?"

"By the girl? It seems that we all felt better as soon as you had her put under. What the hell happened, Kaine? You were supposed to be watching her."

"I was, sir. It came on her right in front of me. She passed out and..." He hesitated, unsure if full disclosure was wise. The captain chose to interpret his hesitation as something else.

"Could she provide any specifics before she collapsed?"

"Ah, no. Er, yes..."

Pavlovich eyed him sardonically. "Which one is it, XO?"

"She...um, described some attributes which might helpful. They appear to be accelerating on an aggressive curve. They will be upon us in less than ten minutes and be travelling at least one-half light speed when they arrive."

"Did she give us any idea of an approach vector?"

"It seems to be the same ship that flushed us out of the *Odyssey* wreck. That would put them on our tail."

"That much from an empathic contact, eh?" Pavlovich turned to the tactical alcove. "Hear that, Gunney? Their acceleration will be doing most of the work for you."

"I could do more if we slowed down. Or stopped..." said the perpetually grumpy cyborg.

"Neither of which is going to happen," said Cora as she entered the bridge. "You're not gonna to tear my baby apart with that kind of manoeuvre just to make your guns hotter."

Hayden smiled to see her up and about, seemingly unaffected by her recent ordeal. "How are you?" he asked as she sat at her station.

"Just a small headache now, and a bruise where I hit my arm when I fainted," she replied. She faced him and lowered her voice so only he could hear. "I had the strangest experience that someone was looking out for me."

He was speechless. She winked at him and returned her attention to her interface.

"All systems green, Cap'n, and awaiting your orders," she said.

"Well, Cora, we *are* going to slow down somewhat," he said. "We need to be more manoeuvrable and can't do that at this speed. Plus, Gunney wants some extra oomph to the rail guns. Fire retros and reduce velocity to fifteen percent of light speed over the next five minutes."

She shook her head, and her hands flew over her console, "That's gonna stress the gravity plating as well as the inertial dampers, but you're the captain, Cap'n."

"Sound emergency deceleration alert. All hands combat conditions. Rangers prepare for potential boarding action," ordered Hayden.

Pavlovich grinned at him. "You seem to be more efficient without your implant, Kaine. I'll make a career officer out of you yet."

He smiled back. "Not if I have anything to say about it," he said. "Sir," he added as an afterthought.

Pavlovich's smile broadened, and he shook his head. "If you're going to be a politician, you need to learn to be a better liar. I think they call it diplomacy."

"Yes, Captain, I'll keep that in mind."

Their banter was interrupted by the intense shaking caused by the retro-engines straining to slow down *Scimitar*. Hayden felt himself grow heavier as the gravity plating struggled to compensate.

The ship jerked to the starboard. Cora's panel lit up.

"We've been hit. Some kind of energy pulse."

"Get a fix on the source and fire rail guns!" ordered Pavlovich.

The deck plates thrummed as all the aft weapons unleashed their projectiles.

The bridge crew waited, anxious for a report from the gunnery officer.

"Anything, Gunney?"

"I don't think so, sir. Hard to tell. We don't know how far behind us they are. The dispersal might not be..."

"Hit registered!" called Hayden from his station. "Readings suggest plasma being released."

A cheer rang up but was cut short by another, more intense shaking of the ship. The pull of gravity fluctuated, along with the lights. Cora's voice rose above the mayhem of automated alert buzzers.

"Direct hit on our engine section. Sub-light engines are out. Guns two and five, damaged. Stabilization out."

"Helm, can you halt our spin?" said Hayden.

"There's no power to manoeuvring thrusters."

"The rotational stress will tear us apart," said Pavlovich.

Kaine strapped himself into his chair as a precaution against the grav-plating going out. If that happened, though, he doubted the harness would do much good. They would all be bloody smears on the bulkheads.

"I need a minute, Cap'n," said Cora, panic in her voice for the first time since Hayden had met her. Her fingers danced across her console. "There, try it now, Helm."

The gravitational pull stabilized as the helmsman fired the manoeuvring engines to stop their death spiral.

"Where did that shot come from?" the captain asked.

"A second vessel is coming from a different vector," announced Hayden, reading the information from his station interface. He missed the efficiency of his LINK.

"Give me ship condition and course," said the captain.

Cora recited the grim news. "On emergency power. Engines and weapons are offline. Structural damage on all aft decks. Hull breaches in sections A through D. We are drifting at eleven percent of light speed with zero spin."

Pavlovich swallowed hard and glanced at Hayden. "Casualties?"

"Six confirmed fatalities and eight unaccounted for."

The captain slammed his fist into the arm of his seat. "And we're as good as dead as well. We can't even see the ghost that killed us."

"I don't think their intention was to kill us, sir, at least, not yet," said Hayden. "They intend to board us."

"How you know this?" said Pavlovich.

"I...I can't explain, sir, but I believe they are after the girl."

At that moment, a loud boom sounded throughout the ship, and it was jerked by contact with something massive.

The captain said, "Get the rangers to the airlocks."

Boarded

RANGER EAGLE SQUAD waited at the entrance to airlock number five.

"I really hope they pick this one," said Ender.

"Be careful what you wish for," said Atan.

"Aww, c'mon, Chief, you've been fixing for a real fight since we came through the light-gate."

She looked at her second in command and grinned.

"That's what I thought," said the corporal, grinning back.

A deafening boom echoed around them.

"It's this one! I just know it."

"Stow it," Atan said, all business. She lowered the visor on her helmet, and he followed her lead.

"You and Tin-key move to the other end of the corridor. We'll trap them in our crossfire. Remember, particle weapons only. Lasers won't work on these bastards. Keep behind the bulkheads."

"Aye, Chief," he said. He and the synth moved to their positions.

She and Win-key retreated the other direction to use another bulkhead for cover. She crouched in a shooting posture as the larger synth assumed a post across the narrow corridor from her.

Another clang of metal rang out. Atan activated her comm link. "Bridge, this is Eagle Squad registering enemy movement at Airlock Five."

The XO's voice replied on her receiver. "Acknowledged. Stand alert. We've got similar activity at Airlocks Two and Four."

"Roger, that. Standing ready," she said.

She noted the time index on her HUD display and glanced at the life indicators of her team. She said a silent prayer that they would all still be active at the end of all this. Though not a religious person, she still believed she should take all the help she could get.

An explosion rattled through the deck plating. Atan trained her weapon at the hatchway.

"Bridge: Eagle Squad; External hull breach at A-Five."

She didn't hear if her message was acknowledged, because a second blast blew open a jagged, gaping hole where the hatch used to be. Inside the dark opening she saw nothing.

Controlling her breathing, Atan flipped through the various visual filters available to her visor. Nothing gave an indication of who or what would enter through the breach. Her eyes never left her display. She didn't believe the Malliac could be completely undetectable.

Then she saw it. A faint distortion twisted the otherwise featureless hole in the wall.

"They have some kind of energy shield!" she shouted while taking aim. All four of the Rangers let loose with their PK 506 projectile weapons. Unable to see their intended targets, all they could do was use everything they had in the hope that the invaders could be killed or injured.

Impacts rippled on the alien shielding, confirming their target location and a focus for them to concentrate their withering fire. Empty shell casings rattled to the floor as they emptied their clips at the unseen foe.

Her enemy's position now reasonably established, Atan raised her arm cannon and fired. A massive explosion shook the deck.

The others followed her lead and unleashed their own weapons to similar effect.

An energy bolt, black as night, flashed from the airlock and slammed into Ender. His armour shattered, and he was hurled ten metres further down the corridor. Before she realized what had happened, a second beam took out Tin-key. Her eyes darted to her readout, but she saw no life indicators for either Ranger.

"Bridge: Eagle Squad is down two. No effect on aggressor with anything." She didn't really think there was anything Ops could do to help her, but it was her duty to report the progress of the engagement."

"Roger, ES. We're going to try something. Turn your gravity compensation to maximum."

She risked a glance at Win-key, who nodded that he had heard the message. She activated her suit's grav-comp and continued to lay down fire at the breach.

The grav plating hummed beneath her feet and her HUD told her that Ops had turned up the artificial gravitation in this section to six times Earth normal. The ripple of the alien shield intensified and dropped closer to the deck.

With a renewed determination, she unleashed a barrage of shells from her arm cannon at the only indicator she had of the invaders' location. After three massive blasts to the shielded specter, the distortion winked out. Atan had no way to know if the enemy was dead, injured, or simply lost its shield cover, so she released another withering round of PK 506 fire until her last clip was empty.

Without warning, a different ripple appeared above where the previous one had vanished, and a black bolt shot from the opening at her. The bulkhead took most of the blast, but she was thrown backward into the wall. Pain wracked her body. She was pretty sure ribs were broken and her shoulder was dislocated. If the servos in her armour hadn't been fried, she still might have been able to put up a fight, but as things stood, she was trapped inside a 500 kg coffin, unable to move or defend herself.

She had a view of the breach in the door. Though she couldn't see the Malliac, she knew it was only a matter of minutes before they took out Win-key and gained access to the ship.

A searing pain exploded in the centre of her skull. She fought to keep her eyes open and tried in vain to lift the arm cannon.

With stars flashing across her vision, she realized she was losing consciousness.

It was over. She had failed.

ISHMAEL GABRIEL ENTERED the infirmary to the sounds of explosions reverberating throughout the ship. He needed to see Stella and took advantage of the battle to leave his quarters to find her.

The medical synth stopped him inside the doorway. "You are not authorized to be here. Please return to your designated emergency station."

"Not without my daughter."

"I realize she is important to you, sir, but she is perfectly fine and safe."

"I don't want her to be alone when they reach here. You hear that noise out there? That battle is being lost. They are coming for her. Let me stay with her in our final moments."

"You are not permitted to be here during a combat alert." It moved forward to escort him out.

Gabriel raised his arms in surrender. "All right, I will go. But first, tell me how she is."

The synth changed its manner. "She rests comfortably and is in no distress."

"I don't believe you. Show me the readouts so I may satisfy myself that is the case."

After a moment of consideration, it said, "Of course. Please come this way to see for yourself."

After it turned to lead him to Stella, he pulled a small unit from his pocket and pressed it against the machine's back. The device emitted a brilliant flash, and the android collapsed to the floor, immobile.

Confident that it was no longer a concern, he advanced to the medical bed where Stella lay. Though under sedation, her brow was wrinkled by some internal anguish.

He deftly adjusted the pumps administering the drugs. "Don't worry, my darling girl. We are leaving here right away."

Shortly, the sedatives flowing into her body were replaced by the required stimulants to bring her out of her coma. A minute after that, Stella opened her eyes and peered groggily at her father.

"Papa? What has happened?"

"The Malliac are here. The soldiers are holding them off and will keep them occupied while we leave, but we must hurry."

She started to sit up and paused to steady herself. "Where are we going?"

He eased her to a sitting position and then permitted her a moment to adjust. "We are getting off this vessel. We will take an escape pod. The star-gate is near, and we will soon be safe."

"What about everyone else?"

Gabriel hesitated. "They aren't coming."

"We're leaving them? They will be killed. He will die."

He assisted her to stand and steadied her while her balance returned. "Yes, I'm afraid they will all perish. It cannot be helped."

Stella started to protest, but her father interrupted her. "There is no more time for discussion. The creatures have breached the hull and are searching for you. We have to go now."

Nodding in resignation, she leaned on him to help her to the doorway. She saw the figure lying on the floor.

"What happened to the medic?"

"It has malfunctioned. We must hurry. The escape pod is only a short distance down the hallway."

Stella submitted and allowed her father to escort her out of the infirmary. They paused in the corridor, and he listened for signs of the battle. Satisfied that the soldiers were still engaging the aliens, he urged her in the opposite direction from the shots and explosions.

She shook her head, and her face wrinkled with pain. "Everyone is afraid, Papa."

"I know, my dear. Try to shut them out, just as I taught you."

She stopped in her tracks and clutched her head. "No. They will kill them. So much hate. So much fear. Make it go away." She sank to her haunches and rocked in misery.

"Stella, please listen to me. I can't carry you anymore, like when you were small. You must walk. I cannot sedate you. You have to fight it for a short time. Soon it will be behind us."

She looked up at him, tears running down her cheeks. As she nodded, her expression reminded him of when she was a child. He helped her to stand. They walked two more steps when Stella straightened up and stared into the space ahead of her.

"No, he mustn't die. He is so afraid."

She looked at her father, intent determination on her face. It was an expression he had never seen. Gone was the trusting little girl he had spirited away to safety so many times in the past. His heart broke at the realization that he had lost her to adulthood, and now he was in real danger of losing her to the enemy.

"Stella, what can you do? We must go before it is too late."

"No, I must protect him."

She closed her eyes and lifted her chin. Her face relaxed. Before Gabriel could urge her on, a sharp pain struck him between his eyes. It grew in intensity until he thought his brain was aflame.

Collapsing to the deck, he looked up at his daughter. Her previously serene face was contorted.

Tears streamed down her face as she said, "Don't worry, Papa. I will drive them off."

Explanations

HAYDEN'S ARMS WERE crossed over his chest, and he struggled to maintain his composure. Across the table from him in the ship's brig was Doctor Ishmael Gabriel. The older man sweated and stared at his manacled wrists resting on the tabletop. Hayden had argued against the restraints, but the captain was pissed off and would brook no discussion on the matter.

Two things kept the scientist from being spaced by Pavlovich. First, the fact that their mission was to retrieve him, and it wouldn't go well if it was learned he'd been thrown out an airlock. And second, because of Gabriel's actions *Scimitar* had been saved. He wasn't sure which reason motivated the captain's mercy more.

Right around the time that Stella was roused from her sedation, two strange and inexplicable things happened. Almost the entire crew experienced debilitating head pain before collapsing into unconsciousness, and the aliens broke off their attack and left.

Hayden recalled the shock of finding himself the only conscious person on the bridge. Desperate, he searched every deck, checking every downed crewman for a pulse or some sign of life. He finally discovered the unconscious forms of Stella and her father in the corridor outside of the infirmary.

Pavlovich wanted her placed into suspended animation, but for the moment she rested, sedated, in the medical centre under armed guard, thanks to some deft negotiation by Hayden on her behalf.

"Doctor, you haven't been truthful about yourself or your daughter. I think it is time we went over the details from the top."

Gabriel tiredly raised his shackled arms in resignation. "I have little choice in the matter, Lieutenant." He forced a half smile, but Hayden remained unmoved.

"How long have you known about Stella's abilities?"

He sighed. "I learned of her special nature when she was a toddler, but I suspected it soon after her birth. Adele, my wife, was pregnant with Stella when we were first working on the ruins of Dulcinea."

"You never mentioned her before. What happened to her?"

Gabriel sank lower into his seat and stared at his hands with a mournful expression. "She died days after our daughter was born."

"Complications of childbirth?"

He shook his head. "The birth was normal...almost painless for Adele. But I believe that was because of her other injuries."

Gabriel's eyes closed, and a tear ran down his cheek. "During the dig, we tripped something. I thought it was a security system, but she believed it was something more...transformative. It trapped her and exposed her to radiation. I now suspect it was a form of dark energy.

"At first, she showed no signs of any injury. We were worried that the child had been affected, but everything checked out normal for both, and we resumed our work.

"During her last trimester, she began to experience horrendous headaches and had vivid, frightening hallucinations. She became overprotective of the baby, not letting me anywhere near her. Soon after, she died."

"I'm sorry for your loss, Doctor. Do you know what the cause of death was?"

"In those days, there was a physician we knew. He was kind enough to perform an autopsy. All Adele's systems were normal except for her brain. Her cortical implant had been destroyed, and she had damage in several regions, but the most significant injury was an altered anterior insular cortex."

"I'm not a biologist. What does that control?"

"Empathy."

"So, the device you triggered damaged her brain?"

"No, it changed it, which in turn impaired her implant. It was her LINK that eventually killed her."

Hayden recalled the severe headaches the rest of the crew experienced during Stella's outbursts. Was he spared because his was deactivated?

"Did you ever examine your daughter's brain after her birth?"

"No, there were no facilities to do anything like that. But I knew something was different when she began exhibiting her abilities, around the age of three."

"Does Stella have a cortical implant?"

"No, and it is my theory that her lack of having one has allowed her to develop her powerful empathic ability. I believe if she possessed a LINK, she would have met the same fate as her mother."

"What has this to do with her connection with the Malliac?"

Gabriel shook his head. "I don't know. The technology that started this is Glenatat. Perhaps it was something they used to defend themselves."

"Forgive me for being blunt about this, Doctor, but why aren't you dead? You lived with Stella for twenty years. I would think that being exposed to her for that length of time would fry your LINK, and your brain with it."

"Her powers were not always so strong. In fact, they have grown since you found us. We remained isolated from others for her entire life. Perhaps her sudden exposure to so many people's emotions at once triggered the growth of her ability. I, myself, experienced pain and collapse like the rest of the crew, and that has never happened before."

Stella's gift was turning into a two-edged sword. On the one hand, she could detect and, seemingly, drive off an invisible and overwhelming enemy. On the other hand, she might end up debilitating the very people she was trying to protect. And her own response to the presence of the aliens was far from benign. She experienced significant distress and had collapsed on more than one occasion. Were her abilities killing her?

Hayden had managed to delay her being put into cryogenic suspension, pending this investigation. Her freedom was going to depend on how much he could learn about how well she could control her power. He realized he was spending whatever trust and goodwill he had earned with Pavlovich since his arrival. He didn't have much latitude and suspected he had even less time. He doubted they had seen the last of that Malliac vessel.

Stella's Fate

THE CREW AND SHIP CAME away from the attack with extensive damage, and the deaths of fifteen crewmen weighed on everyone. But Hayden's thoughts were dominated by another concern: that the crew's collective emotions would adversely affect Stella and justify the captain's desire to put her into suspended animation.

The chief medical synth, Doctor San, was just finishing up Stella's examination when Hayden and the captain arrived at the infirmary. The girl was surprisingly composed and regarded them warily as they entered the room. Pavlovich ignored her and went straight to speak with the physician. While he appeared calm, even relaxed in his interaction with the medical staff, Hayden did not take that as a sign that things would go well for Stella.

"You look nervous, Lieutenant," she said, smiling shyly.

"Well, I suppose you'd know that, wouldn't you?" he said, returning her smile.

"I don't need to be an empath to guess what you're feeling. Your body language is screaming it out loud."

He blushed. "I'm sorry, I just..."

She placed a gentle hand on his arm, and he felt a wave of calmness envelope him like a warm blanket. It took all his effort to gently disengage himself from her touch.

"You're surprisingly calm, Stella. Aren't the strong emotions of the crew difficult for you?"

She took a moment to consider it. "I'm not too experienced with large groups, but when everyone shares the same emotion, I find it less...disruptive."

"How do you mean?"

"You know what it is like to first walk barefoot on a smooth surface? Your feet might feel the initial coolness and texture, but after a short while, you become accustomed to the sensation. You eventually don't even notice the floor...until you step on a pebble or something else."

"So, when a group experiences a common emotion, you grow used to the sameness?"

She nodded.

"And when something unexpected crops up, it's like stepping on a sharp rock for you?"

"Yes, I think so."

"So as long as I keep my crew feeling the same way, you can't harm them?" said Pavlovich, who had joined them, unnoticed.

"I'm afraid you've got it wrong. I'm the one who responds to them."

"Then how do you explain the headaches and our collective collapse?"

"I don't know..."

Kaine said, "It seems to me those things only happened when Stella was in contact with the Malliac."

"Hmmm, that might be so, but when you first experienced them aboard the *Odyssey,* only you fainted. Now, my people are collapsing all over the ship when you connect with the aliens. Why?"

Stella's brow furrowed as she considered Pavlovich's question. "Ever since I first encountered them as a little girl, my reaction to the contact has always been the same. A fear so overwhelming that I would often faint or become so hysterical that my father was forced to sedate me."

"I thought he sedated you so they couldn't locate you." said Hayden.

"Yes, that is true. It seems that once connected to them, they can detect me as clearly as I them. The sedation broke the connection and allowed us to hide."

"So, what was different this last time?" asked the captain.

"I heard the explosions. Everyone was afraid, just like me. I didn't sense any of the crew that time, only the Malliac. I saw their intentions and I became angry and... well, I can only describe it as pushing them away."

"You pushed them away? With your mind?"

Stella nodded.

"And in the process, my people succumbed as well. If you can't influence others, Miss Gabriel, how do you explain that?"

"I can't."

"Not everyone collapsed, Captain," said Hayden. "My LINK isn't active, and I was unaffected."

Pavlovich granted him a skeptical look. "You're saying her push back of the aliens also clobbered everyone's implant?"

"I spoke with her father before we came in here. Some of the things he told me sound related to what happened to Stella's mother." Hayden shared his conversation with them.

"That is consistent with my examination of the young lady," said Doctor San, who had been listening. "I gave her a complete brain scan, and it reveals a substantial anomalous development of her anterior insular and visual cortex."

Pavlovich frowned as he considered everything he had just heard. "Very well, Mister Kaine. I'm prepared to reconsider my position. What line of action do you propose?"

"First, I recommend that we conduct random examinations of some of the crew and compare those scans to their records, as well as my own, since I was not affected."

"I think I see where you are going with this," said Pavlovich.

"But I don't," said Stella.

"My theory is that everyone who had an active LINK will show some degree of deterioration around the implant site," said Hayden.

"And that means for us to take tactical advantage of your abilities, young lady, my crew must give up their LINKs. That is asking a lot of them, Kaine."

Hayden recalled his own feelings of disconnection from the world that he'd enjoyed his whole life. It felt like a part of him had been cut off. He wasn't sure everyone could cope with that loss. "I realize that, sir, but it may be our only defence if the Malliac mount another attack."

"Unfortunately, Mister Kaine," said Doctor San, "deactivating everyone's implant is not possible."

"Why not?" said Pavlovich, "You turned off Kaine's."

"The lieutenant's was simple to deactivate because it was defective since the day it was implanted. His brain compensated for the defect over time. Most of his neural pathways healed themselves some time ago. It is far more complex to turn off a functioning one. We simply do not have the equipment, and if we did, the recovery time for each patient would be weeks."

Pavlovich frowned and regarded Hayden critically. "Alternatively, I can put the girl into suspended animation and take our chances the aliens will not be able to locate us. Or I could simply give her to them."

Hayden's jaw dropped open, and terror was written on Stella's face. Her hand grasped his, and as it did, a cold, debilitating fear washed over him. Realizing what was happening, he released her hand.

"Sir, you can't be considering that option."

"Why not? Our instructions were to retrieve her father. Earth knew nothing of her existence. She is the one the Malliac want so badly. If we let them have her, maybe they'll leave us alone."

"Please don't do that, I beg you." Tears ran down Stella's cheeks. "You don't understand. I saw them the last time. I know what they are like."

"What do you mean you saw them? I thought you were an empath?"

"I... I don't know why, but I saw them. I'm not lying." She looked to Hayden for some sign of support.

"I saw them too, Captain," he said. "When I picked up Stella, after she collapsed, I saw in my mind a vision of an alien ship. I knew it was the Malliac. I felt them as well."

"Her visual cortex and other areas of the brain once believed to be associated with so-called telepathy displayed signs of alteration," said Doctor San. "I can't say for sure, but I would not discount the possibility that what she says is true."

"You're telling me both she and Kaine saw the aliens?" said Pavlovich.

"No, I am saying it is possible she did. I cannot attest to any of the lieutenant's claims."

The captain looked from San, to Hayden, to Stella, confusion on his face. "All right, for a moment let's assume that I believe you two, and you did see the Malliac. Did you get any idea of what they want during your contacts?"

She nodded. "There is a rage that drives them—I don't know how else to describe it. They show an almost instinctive response to us."

"They perceive us as a threat?"

"No, Captain, I don't think it is that. There is a drive that causes them to view us as something to be eradicated."

"Or exterminated," said Pavlovich. "Maybe we are an infestation in their eyes."

"But we've never encountered them before. They showed up and destroyed Dulcinea, unprovoked," said Hayden. "What possible reason would make them want to wipe us out?"

"What causes one invasive species to overwhelm another? They come from a place dominated by dark matter. Perhaps they are so different from us that we will never understand their motivations. Maybe the situation is what the young lady says it is: they have an instinctive aversion to us, like we do to snakes or rats."

The room fell silent.

Stella clung to Hayden. Pavlovich seemed to notice, and his expression softened.

"Don't worry, Miss Gabriel. I will not be turning you over to the Malliac. I have a tendency for hyperbole that occasionally gets the better of me. I'm sorry I frightened you."

Stella's fingers dug deeper into Hayden's arm. She gave Pavlovich a half-hearted nod. "Thank you, Captain."

"We aren't far from the coordinates for your father's wormhole," he said. "We will continue with the plan to try to locate it. Perhaps we'll even find it."

He looked at Stella and failed in his attempt at a reassuring smile. "You might be an asset to us. If you can keep from frying the brains of my crew, I would like to take advantage of your gift."

She looked worriedly to Hayden.

"That would mean you could only see them and warn us. Pushing back might kill us as easily as save us," he said.

She nodded and relaxed a little. "I understand. There is something else you should know, but I want you to release my father before I tell you."

The captain frowned. "You are hardly in a position to negotiate."

She shrugged. "Perhaps you are right, but I saw other things while I was pushing them away. I know where the Glenatat wormhole is, and I am the only one who can lead you through it."

Pavlovich looked at Hayden, and his frown faded until he was chuckling out loud. "She can teach you a thing or two about diplomacy and negotiation, Kaine." He turned to Stella. "Very well, young lady, I will release your father from the brig, and in return you will guide us to the wormhole and knock on the door."

"Thank you, sir."

"However, if you are telling me anything other than the truth, I will put you and your father into suspended animation and keep you there until we arrive at Earth via the closest light-gate. Am I understood?"

"Yes, Captain, I understand you completely," said Stella.

Goodbye and Thank You

HAYDEN ESCORTED STELLA at her request to the makeshift morgue. He was surprised by her insistence and impressed she managed to keep her composure as they entered the hangar bay.

"You're sure about this?"

She nodded and walked ahead of him, making them the only two living persons present. Stella resolutely proceeded to the nearest body laid out on the floor. She stood respectfully silent as he kneeled to unzip the body bag. He pulled open the flaps, revealing the serene face of Corporal Ender.

Her face softened as she regarded the corpse, and Hayden was intrigued when she dropped to one knee and touched the young Ranger's face.

She spoke without looking up. "Did you know him?"

"Yes, for a very brief time. He was a friendly fellow. He served on the team that came across you and your father aboard the *Odyssey*."

Stella nodded but remained silent for a long time. A tear trickled down her cheek. "It's my fault he died."

"No, it isn't. You were under sedation in the infirmary when they attacked. There was nothing you could do."

"I could've been somewhere else," she said, her eyes on the body. "If I wasn't on your ship, he would not be dead."

"You can't say that for sure. He might have been killed when we first encountered them, before we found you. We all could have died that day."

"But you didn't." She looked at him. "Do you believe in fate, Lieutenant?"

He was surprised by the question. "No, I don't. I think our responses to chance events determine our outcome."

It was a practiced statement; his personal attempt to rebel against his father, who considered Hayden's future already determined.

121

"That is a quaint sentiment," she said. "I would like to be as confident as you. Perhaps under other circumstances..." She returned her attention to the corpse. "Was he fated to die as a soldier? How did he go on knowing he was to come to that kind of end?"

"You're assuming he believed in predestination," said Hayden.

"Do you know he didn't?"

He shook his head. "I didn't know him well enough to say."

She nodded and regarded the body again. She kissed his forehead and whispered, "Thank you."

She repeated the same ritual for each of the fallen in the hangar, making no further conversation until they exited and were walking down the corridor.

"You surprise me, Stella."

"How so? Because I kept my cool?"

"Well..."

"I am familiar with death, Lieutenant. Many of the people I knew growing up died at the hand of the Malliac."

When he didn't respond, she looked up at his face.

"Oh, you meant you were surprised that my empathic ability didn't kick into overdrive back there, is that it? I found that place to be peaceful—well, except for your emotions." She regarded him, amused.

"What did you sense from me?"

"Apprehension, mostly. I think you were afraid of how I might react."

He smiled mischievously. "And what am I feeling now?"

She wrinkled her forehead and concentrated on his face. "Many things. Anxiety and fear? I don't know, perhaps the strongest emotion is sexual arousal..." She blushed and resumed walking down the corridor.

Hayden hurried to catch up. "Stella, I'm sorry..."

"No, I should apologize, Lieutenant. I sometimes forget people don't want to share their emotions. Papa tried to teach me about that, but I'm not used to it. It was wrong of me to probe into something that is private."

He touched her on the shoulder and turned her toward him. "But I asked you, and I'm glad you did. I'm relieved to acknowledge those feelings about you."

"Are they really about me, or is there somebody else? I remember the same emotions from you on the night I came to your quarters." Her face was flushed, again.

"There was someone, but I lost her."

"Did she die?"

"No, but I regret that I hurt her. If I could fix things between us, I would, but it's too late."

She put a hand on his, and his nervousness and embarrassment evaporated. "I don't believe in fate. I think there is a role for us to play. Some of us are cursed with knowing our purpose from an early age. Most can blissfully search for it throughout their lives, making do with what they discover and attributing it to destiny. I think we are given the opportunity to accept what the universe, or God, or some higher power sets before us and make the best of things. Some would call it living in the moment."

He felt a comfortable warmth rise up his arm from her hand. She stared into his eyes, waiting for his response.

"Do you..." he swallowed hard, "...live by that philosophy?"

"I do, Lieutenant." She moved closer to him, maintaining eye contact.

He impulsively kissed her. She closed her eyes and returned the kiss.

"It doesn't bother you that what I am experiencing is basically...lust?"

"If I really intend to be in the now, it shouldn't."

She winked and hugged him tightly.

Worried his resolve might fade, he took her by the hand and led her to his quarters.

"TWENTY THOUSAND KILOMETRES to coordinates, Captain," said Ensign Kwok.

"Reduce relative velocity to ten thousand KPH and maintain course." He turned to Ishmael Gabriel. "Any idea how fast we should approach this thing?"

The doctor shook his head. His eyes never left the holographic screen.

Pavlovich mumbled, "I didn't think so." He addressed Hayden. "Anything from the forward drones?"

"Nothing on EM bands; graviton sensors show no anomalous mass. There doesn't appear to be anything there, sir."

"This isn't looking very good for either of you, Miss Gabriel," said Pavlovich.

"It is there. I can feel it," she said, not trying to hide her annoyance with him.

"Well, I can't. Neither can any of my crew, nor can our sensors."

Anger flashed in her eyes. "Did it ever occur to you that it might be as detectable to you as the Malliac? You can't see them, yet you know them to exist."

He slumped into his seat. "Well, we'll be on top of the location in two hours. You'd better figure out some way for us to find it and enter it by then."

Silence fell for the next hour, punctuated only by the noise of the instruments. Hayden studied Stella and her father. She seemed calm, eyes closed and concentrating on whatever it was she searched for. Her father was pale, and his forehead glistened with nervous perspiration. He nervously peered about the bridge until his eyes locked on Hayden's. There was panic in them.

Hayden wandered casually over to Stella, seated next to Ensign Kwok. He leaned over and whispered in her ear, "Your father seems agitated. Is he interfering with you?"

She smiled. "I would be able to feel him from anywhere on the ship. I'm accustomed to him and can tune him out. Only new, unfamiliar emotions from strangers give me problems."

"You'll let me know if you start to experience troubles?"

"What would you do, sedate the person?" A grin spread across her face.

He returned the smile. "I suppose I'll have to, since we need you awake."

"I'm fine, Hayden. I'm used to your crew, and they are performing admirably. I'm not getting any interference from..." Her eyes closed, and a look of intense concentration crossed her brow. "We must make a course correction."

"What?" said Pavlovich, roused from his thoughts.

"The wormhole is no longer in front of us. We'll miss it."

The captain nodded his approval, and Stella relayed the new vector to the helmsman.

After proceeding on their adjusted heading for another thirty minutes, Cora called out from her engineering station. "We've lost drone six."

"Has it malfunctioned?" asked Hayden.

"It was working perfectly. It just stopped transmitting and is not registering with any of the other drones. It's gone."

"Where was the bug when this happened?"

"Approximately 4,300 kilometres ahead."

"Did it enter the wormhole?"

"I don't know, Cap'n. Sensor log shows no anomalous signals of any kind from the drone right up to the time of its loss. No debris spotted by any of the others."

"Do we have a precise location where it vanished?" said Kaine.

"Only to within plus or minus two hundred metres," said Cora.

"Doctor, how large is this star-gate?"

"The records are conflicting and not all that specific, Lieutenant. If I were to speculate, I would say big enough for a Glenatat ship to pass through, so perhaps about half a kilometre in diameter, but that's only a guess."

"With a target that small, we're going to need a more precise fix. Cora, send another drone to where the other one disappeared," said Pavlovich.

"That will be like throwing darts while blindfolded," said Hayden.

"I'm open to suggestions, XO."

"You may not like this one, sir." He turned to Stella. "Do you know how to pilot a ship?"

"Yes, I piloted ours many times."

"Kaine, what the hell are you thinking? There is no way I am going to turn the helm over to a civilian," roared the captain.

Hayden continued to address her. "Could you steer *Scimitar* to the wormhole?"

"Yes, I suppose so, but I'm not familiar with your controls."

"Lieutenant! I told you…"

"Sir, we're attempting to thread a needle we can't see. We could slow down and take pot-shots at it with the drones, but that could take hours, and every minute we spend here makes us vulnerable to the Malliac. I believe letting Stella steer is the fastest way for us to locate it. Besides, it's not like we're making a docking manoeuvre."

Pavlovich ground his teeth, and his meaty hands squeezed the arm of his command chair as he considered Hayden's argument. "Very well, proceed with your plan. Cora, I want you to continue to use the other drones to nail down the position of the wormhole."

"Aye-aye, Cap'n." A big grin spread across her face.

"Helmsman, you will allow Miss Gabriel to pilot the ship, but you will remain alert and be prepared to resume the helm if things go crazy. And Mister Kaine?"

Hayden swallowed nervously. "Yes, Captain?"

"Good thinking."

He relaxed and nodded his thanks as he turned his attention to help Kwok instruct Stella on the basics of *Scimitar's* helm control.

"Cap'n, we might have another problem," said Cora. "I'm detecting that same static on some of the rearmost drones. I think someone might be on our tail."

"Shit!" said Pavlovich.

"Stella," said Hayden, "are you sensing the Malliac?"

"Sort of, but I can't tell for sure. My head is beginning to ache. I've been focused on the wormhole. I can try to find them..."

"No, I have a better idea. What we need is to give them a bit of a scare, so they broadcast themselves," said the captain. "Gunney, can you lay out a spread with our remaining aft rail gun?"

"What am I supposed to shoot at?"

"Target behind us. I don't care if we hit anything, I just want to shake them up."

"Well, I bloody well want to hurt them," mumbled the cyborg as he laid in the coordinates.

"Cora, feed tactical the location of the drones that are registering the static. We may as well try our best to accommodate Gunney," said Pavlovich, smiling at him. The cyborg nodded back emotionlessly.

Within a few seconds, the familiar rumble of the floor plating announced the firing of the rail gun array.

Hayden held his breath in anticipation.

With no warning, Stella pitched forward and gripped her head with both hands. "Oh, my, that certainly got a reaction out of them," she said as she straightened up in her seat.

"Are you okay?" he asked.

She nodded and resumed her efforts at the helm.

"Negative impacts," said Gunney.

Hayden kept his attention glued to Stella, concerned she might be overcome by the approaching aliens. She appeared to struggle guiding the ship but showed none of the distress she had displayed during previous attacks. He wondered if she was getting used to the Malliac.

"I bloody well wish there was a way to tell how far behind us they are," said Pavlovich.

Hayden recalled his experience when she collapsed into his arms. His finger touched the back of her exposed neck. At first, all he noted was the warmth of her skin and her slight relaxation at his touch. Then, suddenly, his mind was filled with the same images of the aliens he'd seen before. This time, however, there was much more than the vision of their ship. He could almost understand what the creatures saw and felt, but it was experienced through a thick, obscuring blanket that limited his ability to confidently interpret. Disconnected snippets flashed before him, and gradually, he thought he understood their meaning.

"They are accelerating toward us. Time to intercept, seven minutes."

"What the hell are you talking about, Kaine?"

Hayden broke his contact with Stella, and the images faded. He struggled to recall details, but they evaporated like an interrupted dream.

"I just shared Stella's link with the Malliac. I got bits of technical detail: velocity, trajectory...intent..." He shook his head to clear it. "They mean to capture us before we reach the star-gate. I got the distinct sense that they cannot cross into it."

"They are afraid of it...of what lies beyond it," said Stella, her attention still directed at the helm.

Pavlovich raised one eyebrow skeptically. "You got that from touching her?"

"We need to increase our speed and get through the wormhole before they reach us," said Hayden.

The captain ordered Kwok to resume control and accelerate. Hayden worried that they would be travelling too fast to make any small course corrections required to pass enter the narrow portal, if that was what Stella led them toward. With the aliens in pursuit, he knew there was little other choice. They would get one shot at this, if they weren't disabled or destroyed by the aliens' weaponry. Their odds of success were depressingly small.

She appeared to struggle as the gap closed between the vessels. Hayden returned his hand to the skin of her neck, and her distress lessened while his anxiety increased. The longer he maintained physical contact with her, the more he was able to separate the jumble of images and emotions flooding into him. The Malliac were present, distinct and foreign, overpowering everything. He sensed their malice, fear, and xenophobic hatred of humanity and was almost overwhelmed by the intensity of it all.

Struggling beneath, he discerned something familiar. Fragile and fighting to remain separate from them, he recognized it as human and realized it was Stella. She did not resist the alien presence, as he fought to do. She focused most of her strength on something weaker. It too was strange and nothing like he had ever experienced, but without the malevolence or emotion of their pursuers. It seemed like a weak lamp seen through a thick fog. He thought it was a manifestation of the Glenatat wormhole she had been leading them to.

Scimitar shook, and he was thrown to the deck. Stella screamed and held her head, eyes wide in terror. Hayden struggled to his feet, and his footing jerked under him a second time. The gravity plating wavered, and he grabbed hold of something to keep from floating off the floor.

Cora shouted above the din of alarms. "Our engines are offline, and the remaining rail gun is inoperative."

"Do we have enough momentum to make the wormhole?" Fear was in Pavlovich's voice for the first time in Hayden's experience.

"Negative," said Kwok. "We've been knocked off course."

They were struck a third time, and the lights and gravity went out. Hayden floated, blind, bumping into loose items and other crewmen. He pushed himself in the direction he knew he would find Stella. Someone latched on to him and pulled him close. The smell of Stella's hair filled his nostrils, and he gathered her into his arms. She shivered, though he didn't know if it was due to her own fear or the collective emotions of the entire crew.

"They're coming," she cried and buried her head into his shoulder. He touched her exposed neck once more and reconnected with her empathic link.

Everything was chaos. He experienced with her the panic and terror of everyone on *Scimitar* and felt himself being overwhelmed. How did she cope with this? He thought it a miracle she had retained her sanity.

Beneath the churning foam of human distress, Hayden sensed a lurking alien presence. He watched her struggle, but the more intense suffering of the people around her wrapped about her like weeds ensnaring a struggling swimmer.

"You have to push them away," he told her.

"I'll harm everyone else. I don't know if they can take it."

"You must risk it, or we will all die."

"I don't want to hurt you, Hayden." The intensity of her own fear almost overwhelmed him, but he struggled to lend her what little calm he could find.

"You can't do anything to me. But they will kill everyone and take you if you don't try to resist them."

"Hold me."

He pulled her close. He fought to retain his own consciousness as he, through his contact with her, sensed every human emotive signal snuffed out. All that remained was the raw presence of the Malliac and Stella. Her energy grew in intensity. Panic rose among the enemy as they experienced her power.

A blinding flash filled his mind.

When it cleared, it was all gone.

Darkness enshrouded the disabled bridge. Stella was limp in his arms. Before she collapsed, while still connected to her, he saw that she had not simply pushed the Malliac away.

He had watched her destroy them.

Taking Stock

CRADLING AN UNCONSCIOUS Stella, Hayden floated, blind in the dark, eerie silence. Only the faint hiss of airflow from the vents told him the environmental system was operational. Nobody would suffocate in the short term, but that was all he was sure of.

He called out but received no reply, not even the moaning of the injured. A jolt of panic shot through him at the thought he might be the only survivor.

His fear was replaced just as quickly by joy as Stella stirred in his arms.

"Hayden?"

"I'm here."

"Where are we? Why is everything so dark?"

"We're still on the bridge. The power is out, along with gravity. We've got breathable air for the moment, but I don't know anything else. I don't even know if the crew still live."

After a moment, Stella's body relaxed. "Everyone nearby is alive."

"How can you tell?"

Her arms wrapped around his neck and hugged him tighter. He relished her warmth, and his anxiousness dissipated.

"Even if someone is unconscious, I can still detect them if they're near me."

"Is anyone here?" There was panic in Cora's voice.

"Cora?"

"Oh, thank goodness. Is that you, Lieutenant?"

"Yes, are you okay?"

"Mmm...yeah, I think so. My head hurts like hell, and I'm hoping the lights are out."

"Yes, they are."

"Whew! That's a relief. What the heck happened? The last thing I remember is the ship taking a hit."

"Kind of hard to explain, but the Malliac are gone. Is there anything you can do about the power or the gravity?"

"Well, some light would help. Did you happen to snag a torch from the emergency kit?"

"No, I haven't begun looking for it."

"Okay, never mind."

He heard a rustling of fabric and other noises as Cora moved blindly about. "Ah, there it is."

"What did you find?"

Her response was the familiar clicking of her workstation keyboard. After several, tense minutes, dimmed lighting came on.

Unconscious crewmen and loose debris floated about the bridge. Those like the captain, who had time to strap themselves in, were tethered to their seats, their relaxed limbs hanging strangely in front of them like those of a person floating in water.

"What is our status, Cora?"

"I can't tell from here. I need to get to engineering." She pushed away from her station and floated to the hatchway.

"Do you want me to come help?"

She grabbed the doorframe and turned to address him. "Excuse me for saying so, sir, but until the cap'n wakes up, you are now in command and your place is here. I'll keep you informed of what I find."

He nodded; grateful the subdued lighting hid his embarrassment. Cora said, "You should strap these people in. If I can get the gravity back online, I'll try to ease it up to normal, but I can't always guarantee a smooth transition. We don't want anyone to get hurt."

"What about others on the ship?" said Stella.

"I imagine most were at their combat stations, but we might find a few who didn't get strapped in. Why don't you come with me, and we'll secure those we find floating loose?"

She tried to push herself away to join Cora, but Hayden held on to her, an unspoken question in his eyes.

"I'll be all right." She kissed him on the cheek and disengaged from his arms. Cora sported a big grin. They left together without her saying a word.

Pavlovich Down

WITHIN AN HOUR, GRAVITY and minimal power levels were restored. Most of the crew regained consciousness with no more than a headache as a reminder of their ordeal. Nine, including Pavlovich, did not awaken and were transported to the infirmary for assessment.

Doctor San worked diligently on the unconscious patients, focusing first on the captain as per Hayden's orders. After two anxious hours, Hayden was summoned from the bridge to the med-bay.

The first face he saw when he arrived was Pavlovich's. He sat upright in his bed, his uniform replaced by a flimsy hospital gown, various tubes and monitors connected to him. Bandages covered his eyes.

"Is that you, XO? Report!" he barked.

Glad to see that Pavlovich's disposition was unchanged, Hayden delivered a concise summary of the status of *Scimitar* and her crew.

The colour drained from the captain's face. "Eight more dead? What section were they in?"

"Simmons and Chen perished when the rail gun was destroyed." He swallowed the lump in his throat.

"And the rest of them?"

"The others who died were in multiple locations throughout the ship."

"What the hell happened?"

"We...we don't know. Doctor San has yet to determine cause of death."

"Where is that quack?"

"Right here, Captain," said the synth, emotionlessly, as if insults from Pavlovich were a normal occurrence. "We've had our hands full dealing with the crew members who've had difficulty regaining consciousness, like yourself."

"All right, then. Let's begin with what you *do* know."

137

The doctor looked to Hayden before answering. "Based on initial diagnostic MRI scans made on all the surviving victims, it appears you all suffered varying degrees of brain trauma in the area surrounding your cortical implants. I'll need further tests to confirm the full extent of any damage, but the long-term prognosis for everyone is favourable."

"How long before I can see?"

The android shook its head. "I don't know yet. It may be days, or weeks."

"Are you serious?"

"Captain, your injury can be repaired, and you will regain your sight, but you will be out of commission for some time."

Pavlovich's jaw flexed while the blood pressure monitor behind him registered a series of shrill beeps. "The girl is responsible for this?" he said, his voice barely audible.

"Yes, sir." Sweat spread under Hayden's arms. "It was our only chance at survival. We'd lost all power, weapons, and gravity and were taking on heavy damage."

"And we're still easy targets for when they regroup and return."

"No, we're not. The Malliac who attacked us are..."

"Yes, Lieutenant? What are they?"

"They're all dead."

"You're sure?"

"I was in physical contact with Stella and saw everything that happened aboard their ship. They all perished."

"She killed them with her mind? Along with eight members of my crew?"

Hayden's shoulders slumped. "Yes."

"Kaine, we're damned lucky she didn't kill us all. Oh, wait...excuse me, but you were always safe, weren't you? Your LINK is disabled. It's every other life aboard that you gambled with."

"Captain, I believe that is out of line," said Doctor San, far more sharply than Hayden had ever heard a synth address anyone. "With the tactical situation as dire as it was, the lieutenant had no other course of action except the one he took. Any other decision would have made this conversation impossible."

"Kaine, I really want to confine you to your quarters for what you did, but I'm forced to admit that your actions saved the ship, and most of our lives." Pavlovich laid his head back against his pillow. "And besides, if I threw you in the brig, I've run out of qualified officers to assume command while I'm stuck here." A slight smile curled up at the edges of his mouth. "Well done, Lieutenant. It appears I may not regret promoting you after all."

Then, just as quickly, his mood became sombre. "I'm making you responsible for the girl. If anyone aboard gets so much as an anxiety attack, I'll put her into suspended animation and throw you in irons."

"You're not in command, Captain," cautioned the doctor.

Pavlovich let his head sink back into the pillow again. "Of course, Doctor." In a more measured tone, he said, "You are commanding now, Mister Kaine. Make good decisions. Our survival depends on you."

Captain Kaine

SCIMITAR's bridge seemed larger without the dominating presence of Pavlovich. Hayden had relieved the captain many times during his duty shifts, but he always felt secure in the knowledge that he was only a comm call away from doing anything too stupid.

Now, with Pavlovich laid up in medical for an indeterminate period, he realized how big the man's shoes were to fill. Every decision he made from this point on was his responsibility, as were the lives of the people under his command. He felt naked.

Pavlovich's appointment of Ensign Kwok as Hayden's second had done little to assuage his trepidation. He imagined every eye was fixed on him, waiting for the inevitable disaster.

He swallowed the lump in his throat.

"Cora, a status report, please." Relieved that his first official order was out of the way, he sat back in the uncomfortable chair and forced his shoulders to relax a bit.

What the hell am I doing here? Only three months ago I was an undistinguished cadet on the admiral's shit list who aspired to a diplomatic career. Now I'm in command of an ancient warship, and this isn't a training drill.

"Cap'n?"

Cora's voice snapped him rudely back to the present. He wondered why the captain didn't answer her until he realized she spoke to him.

Way to go, Kaine.

"I'm sorry, Cora. I was distracted." It was about as lame an excuse as he could have come up with, but he couldn't think of any other way out of the embarrassing situation.

"Do you want the good news first, sir?" Her smile was gracious, as if his faux pas had never occurred. Some did not hide their critical expressions.

"Let's start with the bad," he said, determined to listen closely to every word spoken on the bridge from this point forward.

Cora relayed a litany of far too many inoperative systems that were beyond any hope of immediate repair. As she recited the desperate condition of *Scimitar*, panic seized him. They were all going to die out here, and it would be under his short-lived command.

"I see." Uncertain, he cleared his throat and glanced about, noting the stricken look in the eyes of most of the crew. Only Gunney seemed to take the damage report in stride.

"What is the rest?"

"Environmental systems are fully operational, and gravity plating works on only about half the decks. Navigation control and manoeuvring engines are functioning, and one of the main drives is relatively undamaged. It will be up and running in about four hours. Unfortunately, we won't be able to make any better than one percent of light speed with the rest of them offline."

"How long to effect repairs?"

She regarded him, confused. "Cap'n, there is no way to repair our damage outside of a space dock facility."

Hayden was stunned. Up to this moment, he had experienced Cora as a magician who only needed time to make everything aboard the dated hulk hum along smoothly. She worked a miracle before using whatever scrap parts she scrounged up and put to creative use. It never occurred to him that some things might be beyond her ability to fix.

Everyone seemed to be watching him, waiting for him to make the decisions and give the commands that would save them. How the hell did Pavlovich survive in the captain's chair all these years? His respect for the big man increased by the second.

"Navigation report, please, Mister Kwok." Time and data were what he needed now. Gather as much information as possible before deciding. "How long will it take us to get back to the Mu Arae system?"

"You want us to go back *there*?" she said.

Hayden realized how idiotic his request sounded. More important-ly, however, was Kwok's apparent challenge. If he knew anything about command, he understood the necessity to nip that kind of thing in the bud, or there could be a mutiny before the end of the shift.

"It was an inquiry, Ensign Kwok, not a statement of intent. I want to know *everything*. Now, please answer my question." He hoped he'd put enough authority into his voice.

The pilot snapped up straight in her chair. "Yes, sir." She hurriedly checked her console before answering. "At our best speed we would reach the planet Dulcinea in ten months."

"Thank you. We clearly don't want to make that our first choice, es-pecially with the Malliac looking for us."

A few faces showed some relief.

Emboldened by his minor victory, he continued. "How far are we from the wormhole?"

Kwok again referred to the console. "Our position is stable, and we are now at zero relative motion to our original target coordinates, though we've drifted ten thousand kilometres from it since the attack."

It was hardly a choice. Going back to Mu Arae in the hope that they might somehow repair the jump-gate was risky. They would never sur-vive another attack, and he was pretty sure they were not forgotten by the aliens, based on his brief glimpse into their intentions through Stel-la's connection.

It was impossible for *Scimitar* to continue to the nearest colony planet. At one percent of light speed, they would all be dead before the ship arrived.

The only other available option was the Glenatat star-gate, though that path was fraught with far too many unknowns. Assuming it even existed, they still had to pass through it in one piece. Even if they accomplished those impossible challenges, they still had to hope whomever lay on the other side of it was less hostile than the Malliac, if they found anyone at all. They could just as easily discover themselves floating far from any habitable system somewhere across the galaxy.

"Set a course to take us back to the wormhole, Mister Kwok. As soon as the engine repairs are completed, we will get underway."

Finding the mythical Glenatat home world was their only chance. If any decision he made was going to doom them, he wanted to make the one that would give them the most hope.

A Boost of Courage

HAYDEN DECIDED TO TAKE advantage of the repair time to seek out Stella. They had not spoken since the attack twenty hours before, all their time and energies consumed by the chaotic aftermath. Though well trained and no strangers to emergencies, the crew of *Scimitar* had never faced such a dire situation.

With all the losses, their complement was down by almost a third. Those deaths and the injuries sustained by the survivors, coupled with their extensive damage, meant repair and recovery operations would take far longer than anyone wanted.

He didn't require Stella's ability to discern how everyone was coping. Everywhere he went, he saw the same thing in everyone's eyes: shock and the accompanying fear they might be attacked again before they were ready, perhaps finished off for good by the Malliac.

He tried his best to reassure those he spoke to and keep morale up, but this was a seasoned crew with far more spacefaring experience than he. Everyone was acutely aware of how precarious the situation was. He felt like a naive fool, hopelessly in over his head.

Worse still, they didn't trust him. He could tell by the way they responded to him, by the slight hesitation when asked a question or given direction. While ready to go along with indulging the captain's appointment of him as first officer, they now questioned that decision. With Pavlovich out of commission and the ship in such a desperate situation, he agreed they had reason to doubt his untested leadership.

Stella was assisting in the infirmary; he found her taking inventory of the depleted supplies. She looked exhausted, having worked continually since the gravity was restored and the injured began flowing into Medical.

"Hayden, is everything all right? You look terrible."

Until her comment, he hadn't felt the strain of the past twenty-hours.

"I'm okay. Nothing a few stimms can't address."

"I'm sorry, but we've run out of stimulants."

"I was kidding." He offered a weak smile. "Well, I think I was. Some strong coffee will do."

"You're exhausted. Why don't you take a rest?"

"I can't afford to while the crew is working their asses off." He scanned around the room. "It looks like things quieted down here, though. You should take advantage of it yourself and get some sleep."

It was her turn to smile weakly at him. "I feel the same as you. Besides, I don't think I could after what happened."

Hayden soberly recalled the horrific visions. He suspected that what he shared with her was only a fraction of her experience. "Perhaps later, when this is behind us..."

His hand located hers, and their fingers intertwined. He looked into the dark, blue ocean of her eyes, and his fatigue, doubt, and fear lifted. He didn't know if his relief came from an empathic connection to her or something else, and he didn't care. He wanted to lean forward and kiss her, but a clatter behind them reminded him of where they were.

Stella released his hand and stepped away, wincing in pain.

"Are you okay? Is it the Malliac?"

"No," she said, shaking it off with an unconvincing attempt to smile. "It was just the intensity of your..." She placed a gentle hand on his shoulder. "What you—we—shared, was in sharp contrast to what the rest of the crew are experiencing. It took me by surprise. I'm sorry."

"Please, don't apologize." He paused to glance about the med-bay at the injured. "I should have been more sensitive to you and everyone else."

He sighed; the burden of command once more pressing down fully upon him.

"I came down here to tell you we are getting underway for the wormhole in a few hours. You'll be needed on the bridge."

"I will be there, Captain."

He didn't think he could get used to being called that. He wanted Pavlovich to recover and rescue him from the danger of screwing everything up irrevocably.

Stella stood on her toes and kissed him on the cheek. "I'm confident you will do fine."

He regarded her; an eyebrow raised.

She smiled again. "I don't read minds, Hayden. Your doubts are written all over you for anyone to see. You must believe in your ability to succeed, if not for yourself, then for the sake of everyone else. They need you to be strong."

"I've never been in a situation like this..."

"My father and I have. We'll be here for you to draw strength from. If we could make it through all those years, you and your crew with this mighty ship will survive this."

He didn't know if it was because of her words or her faith in him, but he no longer felt anxious. He kissed the top of her head.

"I'll see you in three hours."

The Wormhole

ONCE MORE, *Scimitar*, with Stella at the helm, slowed on its approach to Gabriel's coordinates. The viewer showed a vast expanse of stars. All operational chatter had ceased, and a tense silence hung like a smothering cloud.

Hayden shot an inquiring glance toward the tactical officer. Gunney answered solemnly, "No sign of the Malliac on the long-distance surveillance systems."

He returned his attention to the screen, only to catch the eye of his nervous second, who had relinquished her station to Stella. Kwok shook her head, apprehension flashing in her brown eyes.

Hayden cleared his throat and announced, "Maintain course and speed, helm."

Even without being an empath, he was certain everyone shared Kwok's doubts. He only hoped everyone's negative emotions didn't affect Stella's ability to locate the wormhole.

Kwok pointed at the viewer. "There!"

A subtle distortion of the star field, like the reflections of the night sky on a rippling pond, was the only indication something lay ahead.

"Science station, what do you read?" asked Hayden.

Cora answered. "A two percent increase in neutrino density, Cap'n. Also, elevated X-ray and gamma ray output from the centre of the distortion, but nothing lethal."

"Helm, reduce speed by one quarter." Confidence was now more evident in his voice. "Give us a little time to see how big the door is."

"Not sure that's even what it is, sir," said Cora, her normally ebullient disposition noticeably diminished.

"That's what your bugs are going to tell us. Send them in."

"Aye, Cap'n," she said, her enthusiasm returning as she resumed her engineering station. Hayden suppressed a smile.

The distorted region of space grew as the ship seemed to inch its way toward it. The tension on the bridge was palpable, with everyone not otherwise occupied riveted to the anomaly in rapt silence.

Cora's voice broke the spell. "We just lost a bug. I think that's the wormhole, Cap'n."

"Is there enough information to tell us how far away and how big it is?"

Cora busied herself. "It is two hundred and eight kilometres dead ahead, sir. The edges of it are diffuse, but it is approximately fourteen hundred metres in diameter."

"So, no risk of scratching the paint, then?" said Hayden. When nobody so much as smirked, he gathered his thoughts and considered the next course of action.

Every eye was on him, waiting for him to decide what to do. Except he had no idea what the potential consequences of that decision looked like. Every option before him only varied in the degree of uncertainty, and none of them was guaranteed to be danger-free. There was a significant chance nothing would change the odds of their survival. How did Pavlovich manage to do this for most of his long career, knowing that almost every day, a wrong choice could kill everyone? He had a new appreciation for the man.

His decision made, he swallowed the lump in his throat and silently prayed it was the right one. "Take us through the anomaly."

The tension built as the ship slowly advanced on the wormhole. Hayden wondered if his shared experience with Stella had made him more attuned to those around him.

As the bow of *Scimitar* contacted the spatial distortion, he held his breath, hoping he didn't commit them to oblivion.

The lighting flickered before the bridge was plunged into darkness.

"Cora?" he said into the blackness, raising his voice above the murmur of the others.

"Give me a moment, Cap'n. There was a power fluctuation."

On her last word, the lights came back on.

"See? There was nothing to worry about," she said, like a reassuring mother.

Hayden returned his attention to the viewer, which was coming back online, along with all the other systems. His mouth dropped open as the hologram filled with millions of bright stars, so thick they appeared as almost a solid wall.

"So many of them," said someone.

He dragged his eyes away. "Where the hell are we?"

"Um...on it sir, but I'll need a few minutes to recalibrate the computer," said Kwok, who had relieved Stella from the helm.

Noting in everyone the same degree of distraction that had enraptured him a moment before, he called out, "System checks, all stations, ship-wide."

The spell broken; the crew hurried to comply with the order. Hayden moved to the science station and reviewed the data the AI had accumulated since their arrival.

He recited the summary, "Elevated levels of X-rays, gamma rays, neutrino emissions, graviton particles..."

Kwok interrupted his litany. "Preliminary positioning places us near the galactic core, somewhere in the 3 KPC spiral arm."

"What? Are you sure about that?"

"I'm not certain about anything, sir, except that we are no longer anywhere close to Mu Arae. The computer is choking on the stellar data. It will take some time to calibrate to known star charts. It may be three hours before we establish a more precise location."

At least we are in the same quadrant of the galaxy, thought Hayden, *as if that is going to help us. We are even farther from home than before. What did I do to us?*

"Cap'n," said Cora, concern in her voice, "the wormhole has vanished!"

He rushed to Cora's station to look over her shoulder at the readouts.

"I lost contact with the last of our bugs, and when I went to look for them, they were gone, along with any sign of the anomaly."

The normally subdued murmur of bridge activity ruptured into a chaotic flurry of questioning voices either trying to gain his attention directly or merely asking of whomever would listen. Stella rocked in pain. Her hands covered her head as she fought to defend herself from the overwhelming emotional storm. Hayden could see the situation slipping into pandemonium. He needed to get control before it was too late.

"QUIET, EVERYONE!"

His outburst had the desired effect. They all stared at him. He only had a few seconds to capitalize on their shock.

"You are the crew of the *Scimitar*, a proud, long-serving ship of the line. I expect you all to perform your duties with the same degree of courage and discipline you have displayed in the past."

"What are we going to do, sir?" somebody said. Grumbles of assent began to rise in volume.

"Who asked that?" He stood to better see and be seen.

Crewman Brennan slowly stepped forward and raised his hand. Hayden recognized him as the one who had voiced initial objections to his appointment as XO. He directed his reply to him but intended it for everyone.

"To answer your question, I'm not sure what we are going to do. Yet. This situation is well beyond what anyone has experience with, so we will need to work together to keep things running and find a solution."

"But, sir," said Brennan, "when will the captain be back?"

Hayden frowned. "I am now in command, and I expect you to show me the same trust and respect you showed him. Is that understood?"

Murmurs bubbled up. He thought heard someone mutter, "Pavlovich never would have led us into this mess."

He saw several heads nod in agreement. The seeds of a mutiny were being sown, and he felt as if he walked in shifting sand, unable to gain a solid foothold. He stood a good chance of being deposed before he could even register his first log entry.

A heavy footstep clanked behind him, and he turned to see Gunney outside of his alcove. Standing at his full height, the cyborg scanned the bridge with his menacing artificial eye. One hand hovered over his holstered side arm.

The hatch opened, and two Rangers entered. They directed their attention to the gunnery officer.

"Is there anything we can do, Captain?" inquired Gunney.

Hayden released his held breath. Calling armed reinforcements was a bit heavy-handed, but he was grateful for their support, nonetheless.

"Thank you. Please instruct your men stand by."

He was conflicted. On the one hand, since his arrival he had worked hard to earn the acceptance and respect of the crew. He regarded many of them, if not as friends, at least as amicable comrades. It was becoming apparent that any such goodwill did not extend itself into confidence in his abilities as captain.

As far as they all were concerned, he was untested. Hell, they all had more experience than he. But Pavlovich had put him in command, making it abundantly clear it was up to Hayden to sink or swim. If he could not garner their compliance through respect, he would have failed. Then he would be forced to use other means to establish his authority.

Standing taller, he said, "I need a complete system check."

As if a switch had been flipped, everyone snapped to their duties. Hayden looked over to Gunney and nodded his thanks. The old Ranger returned a grim-faced salute and resumed his post in his alcove.

As he took his seat, he caught a glimpse of Cora tending to Stella, who appeared exhausted from the torrent of emotional energy that had broken over her. Both women smiled at him in open relief that things had resolved well. He returned their smiles, but his stomach was twisted in knots.

He didn't try to delude himself. The timely arrival of the Rangers prevented something ugly from developing. It was a short-term solution at best. Their support was provisional, especially given the unprecedented situation they found themselves in.

The earlier, muttered complaint burned in his ears. He was no Pavlovich and under normal circumstances would have no business sitting in the command chair. He needed to earn their respect, and quickly.

Things were bound to get worse, and without everyone pulling together, there was no way they would all come out of this alive.

Crew Uneasy

HAYDEN EXITED THE MEDICAL facility, far more keyed up than he had been on entering. His hope was that conferring with Pavlovich would prove helpful in the tense situation he now found himself in. From the beginning of his reluctant assumption of command, he had looked to the captain to provide mentorship through the rough parts.

"Consider yourself lucky Gunney had your back," was all the help Pavlovich offered.

For every question he asked the old fool, he only received vague, backhanded affirmations he'd somehow stumbled across the right decision. It was infuriating, and he wondered if the man hadn't suffered more severe brain damage than the doctor was willing to admit.

Perhaps Pavlovich realized their situation was completely beyond hope and truly had no insight to offer. After thirty years commanding a warship on the frontier, Hayden had hoped his mentor would be able to say something more encouraging than "you dodged a bullet on that one, didn't you?" Maybe he was surprised the ship hadn't blown up by now and had no other way to express his relief.

Hayden had never aspired to a long-term military career. His plan always was to serve only enough time to qualify for a transfer to the diplomatic corps. The DC would not consider him without some service, even if it were only time served safely behind a desk. It was considered a rite of passage Hayden was prepared to endure to achieve his ambitions.

The responsibility for the survivors on *Scimitar* was too much, and the sooner he could rid himself of the burden, the better. The problem was there was nobody among the present crew qualified or capable of assuming command in his stead. If a mutiny were successful, they would all be doomed, if not from the unknown hazards in this region of space, then from the inevitable infighting to see who would lead. Like it or not, with his academy training, he was the most qualified person aboard and the crew's best chance of getting out of this mess.

One of the few useful outcomes of the meeting with Pavlovich was his suggestion to deploy security at critical locations. Though reluctant to rely on heavy-handed tactics, Hayden could think of no alternative. He seemed to have earned the loyalty of Gunney, and as a result, the rest of the Rangers. He would be a fool to not employ whatever allies he had to maintain order. Until the captain's recovery, like it or not, he was in charge. It was time to start acting like it, or there would be no ship to hand back.

Unlike Pavlovich, he had no desire to hold meetings in his tiny quarters. Since there was no formal meeting room aboard, he commandeered a corner of the mess hall to serve as one. He entered to find Ishmael Gabriel bent over a collection of charts, maps, smart documents, and old-style paper notebooks. The man's entire life's work lay spread across a table. Hayden hoped he would one day be able to show as much for his efforts.

"It has been two days, Doctor. What can you tell me?"

Gabriel looked up, confusion on his face. "It should be here."

"It would be helpful if I knew what you were speaking about."

"According to my studies, this is the location of the Glenatat home world. All their star-gates should lead back to it."

"There isn't a star system within five light years of us, Doctor."

"I know, I know. I just don't understand why not. There was no ambiguity in my translations."

Hayden leaned on the table and let his eyes drift across the complex notes and strange hieroglyphs. He could only take the scientist at his word.

"Well, the reality is that either your source is wrong, or you've misinterpreted the record. Now I need you to search through your data to find us anything else we can use."

"My translation is *not* incorrect. Everything I predicted from the records was proved correct: the Malliac, their nature, the star-gate. How can all that be right and the most important detail not be? I need more time."

"There is no more time, Doctor."

"What do you mean?"

"We may have another day or two before things turn ugly on this ship. For now, the crew is preoccupied with ongoing repairs, but they are not happy. I need to provide them with a plan of action that at the very least appears like it has a chance of getting us back home. If that doesn't happen, we could both find ourselves spaced before the week is out."

The colour drained from the scientist's cheeks. "What can I possibly do?"

Exasperated, Hayden flung one of the diagrams to the floor. "I don't care, Doc. Look for another wormhole or figure out a way to open up the one we passed through and get us back to our part of the galaxy."

"But the Malliac are there..."

Before he could respond, the door to the mess hall opened and Warrant Officer Atan entered. Her head was still bandaged, but the doctors had cleared her for duty. Hayden had made her head of security. She approached, warily regarding the doctor. She spoke quietly into Hayden's ear.

Nodding, he said, "Tell them I'll be right there."

As she spun on her heel and hurried from the room, a confused Ishmael Gabriel said, "What is it?"

"Three vessels of alien configuration are on rapid approach to us."

"The Malliac?"

"I don't think so. These ships are visible."

Gabriel's eyes widened. "The Glenatat found us."

"Well, if they have, I hope they're friendly and you know of a means to communicate with them, otherwise a mutiny will be the least of our worries."

The Glenatat

"SOUND GENERAL QUARTERS. Bring all available weapons on-line."

Although he'd heard the order several times since his arrival on *Scimitar*, the words sounded strange coming from his mouth. Hayden hardly noticed the flurry of acknowledgements from the bridge stations as he focused his attention on the main viewer.

Still more than one hundred thousand kilometres away, the three approaching alien ships were far closer than necessary for full-scale resolution by *Scimitar's* scopes. Even at this distance, every detail of their flawlessly beautiful hulls was discernible. Each one consisted of a central sphere, invisibly suspended inside an encircling nest-like globe of metallic rings. No obvious front, back, top, or bottom was apparent. They seemed more like metal-girded bubbles than interstellar spacecraft and looked anything but warlike.

He was not about to allow his guard to drop based on that kind of interpretation, however.

"Beautiful." Ishmael Gabriel's rapt attention to the holo-image told Hayden more than the man's admiring comment.

"I assume you recognize these ships as Glenatat, Doctor?"

"Oh, they are more magnificent than I could ever imagine from the record descriptions. Yes, Captain, they are indeed."

"Are they hostile?"

"Whatever do you mean?"

"They likely have never encountered humans. Will they roll out the welcome mat, or are these the bouncers?"

The scientist was nonplussed. "I... I surely don't know."

Hayden blew out from puffed cheeks and turned back to the approaching ships. "I was afraid you would say that. I'm betting, based on their apparent lack of any form of engines on their structure, that their weapon systems are equally weird and formidable."

"I would think so, Captain. The Glenatat established a galactic empire twenty thousand years before humanity learned how to cultivate crops."

"I don't suppose they can be expected to use anything as primitive as radio waves?"

Gabriel shrugged.

"Well, I guess we should try anyway," said Hayden. "See if you can get any kind of response out of them, Ensign Bates."

"Captain, there is only twenty percent power on the forward lasers," said Gunney. "Our remaining operational rail gun is at the ready. Optimal effective range is five thousand kilometres."

If these beings were as advanced as Gabriel suggested, *Scimitar's* weaponry would probably prove useless at any distance.

The hatch opened, and Stella squeezed through the opening, only to be stopped by the imposing figure of the security chief, who guarded the bridge. Hayden waved to Atan, who permitted the girl to enter. She approached with a worried expression.

"How are we doing?" he asked quietly.

She regarded him, puzzled, before realization set in. "Everyone is anxious, but you didn't need me to tell you that." She smiled weakly.

He returned her smile before returning his attention to the viewer. "Time to intercept?"

"They'll be on top of us in just under a minute," said Cora.

"Keep the bugs well away from them. No sense letting them think they're being attacked."

"Aye, Cap'n."

True to Cora's prediction, the three massive ships arrived and encircled the *Scimitar*.

"As if we had any chance to escape in our condition," said Hayden. "Mister Bates, anything on the comm?"

"If they heard us, sir, they haven't let on."

The atmosphere was deathly still, as if everyone was afraid to breath. Two minutes passed without a word being uttered. The alien ships hung in space, giving no indication if they were friend or foe.

"Perhaps they intend to bore us to death?" muttered Hayden. Someone stifled a laugh.

Stella seemed calm.

"Are you getting anything?" he asked.

"Nothing," she said, "almost as if nobody is out there."

"Captain," said Kwok. "We seem to be moving."

He examined the screen for any indication of relative motion. Seeing nothing, he rushed to the science station and reviewed the AI log. Their distance to all three vessels had not changed since their arrival. The logs showed some minor increase in graviton field density, but that could easily be attributed to the presence of the three massive ships.

"Ensign Kwok, how did you come to that conclusion?"

"Sir, we're so distant from the nearest star that it took some time to notice, but the navigation computer just confirmed we have moved almost fifty thousand kilometres from our last measured position. It isn't drift, either. Those ships are moving right along with us, and we are accelerating."

"Damn it! Of course. We are being towed. They must be using graviton technology to move us."

"Captain, I can attempt to disable one of them with a pulse from the laser cannons," said Gunney.

Hayden studied the image of the alien ships on the viewer. They appeared so benign. "Stand down. If they meant us any harm, we wouldn't be able to do much about it. They want us to go somewhere, so for the time being, we will cooperate."

The cyborg grunted, clearly not pleased.

"However," Hayden added, "maintain full alert status and order the Rangers to armour up, just in case somebody tries to board us, uninvited."

A satisfied grin spread across his ugly face. "Aye, Captain, consider it done."

"Mister Kwok, have you any idea of our course?"

"Still compiling the data, but it appears we are being dragged back to where the ships came from."

"Is there anything in that direction?"

"Not even a star, sir, which is really weird."

"How do you mean?"

"Well, with the stellar density in this part of the galaxy, you would be hard pressed to find a single region that is empty of stars, and yet that is exactly where we are heading."

Hayden adjusted the viewer. There, in the centre of the image, amid a solid wall of starlight so thick that it was difficult to make out individual points of light, lay a dark hole in space.

"And the even stranger thing is," added Kwok, the tension in her voice rising, "that particular area is growing in size."

Hayden stared at it, trying unsuccessfully to see what the helmsman had described. Frowning, he considered a potential action that might seem confrontational to the aliens, but he had to know if he was right.

"Cora, deploy the bugs forward and direct their sensors at the black hole." He winced at his poor choice of words. "I want an estimate of size and distance."

Returning to the science station, he examined the logs. No X-ray or any other kind of radiation emission came from the region, and gravity readings showed insufficient mass for it to be a singularity.

"Cap'n," said Cora, "preliminary data coming in now. That thing is almost two hundred and fifty million kilometres in diameter. We are about twenty light-hours from it and closing at ninety-three percent of light speed."

He looked incredulously at her.

"And our remaining engine isn't even warmed up," she added.

A loud murmur arose while Hayden rechecked the data. He leaned back against the console, laughing.

The buzz of conversation ceased as everyone regarded him, puzzlement on their faces. Seeing them, he got control of himself, lest they think he'd gone off the deep end.

"Sorry, but I think I know where they are taking us." He pointed at the growing black region on the display. "That is a Dyson sphere."

The Dyson Sphere

EIGHTEEN HOURS AFTER the Glenatat began towing the *Scimitar*, they neared the Dyson sphere. Its enormity blotted out everything before the ship. Hayden ordered all astrometric scopes and ship's instruments trained on the impossible artificial structure. He seriously doubted they could record information across a third of it. What they did observe, however, fascinated him.

They were now close enough for the diffuse starlight of the galactic core to reveal surface detail. It was clearly ancient, scarred and pitted with the markings of asteroid and comet impacts. None of the spectrographic readings gave any indication what it was composed of. Hayden couldn't begin to imagine the level of technology required to construct it. Its diameter would enclose the orbit of Mars, if it had been around the Sol system.

One observation made during their approach disturbed him. Marring fifteen percent of its surface and wrapping around to the back of it was an enormous, circular scorch mark. It looked like something the size of a major planet had impacted against the structure.

He had no way to confirm his notion, but Hayden suspected the scar was of relatively recent origin, seeming more artificial than natural. He wondered who or what might be capable of mounting such a massive assault and worried the Malliac were responsible. He despaired over humanity's pathetic inability to defend itself against them.

When it seemed like they were going to be driven into the surface by the three alien ships, an opening large enough to swallow a thousand *Scimitars* appeared, and they were ushered inside. The encasing structure was as thick as the diameter of the Earth, and the claustrophobic passage through it lasted over a minute.

When they emerged on the other side, they were dazzled by a wondrous sight. What should have been the empty blackness of interplanetary space was filled with the glow of an enclosed red giant sun. Hayden had the impression of being inside an impossibly large room, rather than a solar system.

This star was billions of years older than humanity's own, and the unimaginable technology around them testified to an advanced race, perhaps as superior to mankind as humanity was to single-celled organisms. Hayden wondered if it was even going to be possible to communicate with them, or if they would recognize humans as sentient. They might simply view the crew as an infestation to be exterminated.

Scimitar was ushered toward a small planetary body suspended within the ruddy interior. It was only as the distance between them closed that Hayden realized it was an artificial structure constructed of the same materials as the outer wall. It seemed tiny against the enormity of the sphere. Scimitar's instruments established it as the size of Earth's moon.

This object, however, was pristine and reflected a ruddy glow from its grey, matte surface. The station, as Hayden dubbed it, was encrusted with what looked like buildings.

An opening formed in the side, and they were escorted inside by the three ships.

The interior was far different. The inner side of the shell was also covered in an endless city. Bridges extended for kilometres, forming a network converging at a spherical module in the centre of the space. Multiple small, strange-looking things that looked like bugs were attached to it. Some of the objects detached and swiftly exited through other openings like the one they had transited.

"This looks like some kind of dock," said Hayden, breaking the long silence that had enveloped the bridge. He turned to the gobsmacked Gabriel and said, "Is any of this familiar to you, Doctor?"

"The records on Dulcinea were woefully incomplete. I knew there would be a civilization here, but I had no idea..."

"Well, we must be interesting to them," said Cora, "otherwise, why bring us here?"

"Maybe we were collected, like a strange insect." Images of Hayden's biology class dissection labs sprang to mind. "I'm bothered that they haven't tried communicating with us."

"Communication requires some common reference," said Gabriel. "Humans use sounds, facial expressions, and body language on multiple levels. We've developed sensitivity to these forms over millions of years of evolution."

"But the Glenatat, or even the Malliac, might not be able to communicate with us because they do not share our adaptations to do so?"

"That is one theory, posited by the more pessimistic."

"You have a different idea?"

Gabriel looked at Hayden like he was a slow student who didn't understand the obvious. "Of course. I've dedicated my life to translating the writings left by this race on Dulcinea. The very fact that their written records are decipherable means we share a basis to establish contact, even if it is only by writing."

He fixed Hayden with a hard look. "Humanity has become complacent about communication, having so long spoken only among ourselves. We advanced our technologies along one narrow path so that our intercourse is now encoded in agreed artificial protocols."

He gazed at the image on the viewer. "We forgot about the power of the written word, preferring digital media in the delusion that it is the most sophisticated means of congress. If we were to lose our technology, centuries of human thought and achievement would be lost forever."

He turned back to Hayden; his eyes ablaze. "But the Glenatat, far more advanced than we, understood this. That is why such an elder civilization as theirs left a permanent written record, likely on every world they occupied. My colleagues scoffed at my ideas. But our recent experiences, everything before our very eyes proves those fools wrong. That we located them through their records is a testament to our commonality with them."

His passion cooling, he said, "Yes, Captain, we can communicate with them, using the alphabet they left for us in the Mu Arae system."

"Well, Doctor, you will soon put your theory to the ultimate test." Hayden indicated the growing image on the viewer. "It would appear we have arrived. I'm hoping they didn't bring us here to tack us up on a collection board, so you better figure out the easiest way to ask them to take us to their leader."

Welcoming Committee

THE ONLY INDICATION they had docked with the hub was the departure of the three escorts. As they accelerated away, Hayden wondered about their weaponry, if any. Would the *Scimitar* have provided any kind of significant resistance? Hopefully his decision to passively assume their superiority didn't merely delay their own destruction. After all, even an insect can sting its captor.

The truth was, going along with the Glenatat ships had been the only chance for survival. Trapped in an uncharted part of the galaxy, so far from home, return was impossible. Damaged beyond repair, *Scimitar* was doomed without help from someone. Now, his entire gamble came down to trusting an eccentric scientist's controversial theories.

The Glenatat were perceptive enough to determine the location of one of *Scimitar's* docking ports. Hayden thought of stationing some heavily armed rangers at the airlock but decided that might send the wrong message. Instead, after discussion with Security Chief Atan, he agreed to place her soldiers behind the first bulkhead and out of line of sight, where they still had a defensive tactical position. If everything went to hell when they opened the hatch, survivors could testify at his court-martial that he tried to defend *Scimitar*. If it came to that, he didn't anticipate there would be any. On that more likely scenario, he'd ordered Cora to stand by in the engine room. As a last resort, she would collapse the confinement field around their microsingularity and destroy the ship.

Hayden, Gabriel, and after very strong insistence by both her and her father, Stella, were to be the only visible greeting committee for whatever lay beyond the docking port hatch. The doctor brought an elaborate board, crammed with Glenatat symbology to show to whomever they admitted. He hoped the aliens had eyes with which to read the note the scientist insisted was a message of peace and goodwill.

Anxious, Stella shifted her feet and absently rubbed her hands together.

Hayden asked quietly, "How are you feeling?"

"Are you serious? I'm pretty much the same as everyone aboard the ship."

He worried his order that her sedative doses be discontinued might be a mistake. He wanted her at her full potential if the Glenatat proved similar to the Malliac, but Stella continued to insist she could not detect anyone but the crew.

Stella's cold fingers intertwined with his, and she looked up at him. "I'm sorry for being so snippy. Don't worry, I won't collapse on you."

He squeezed her hand and forced a reassuring smile, but he knew she could see through him. His heart pounded wildly, and his uniform stuck to him from perspiration.

He had no idea what he was doing. Only gut feel could guide him in whatever was going to happen. Nothing in his academy training had prepared him for anything like this. The lives of everyone depended on his ability to make the right choices, and he couldn't even control his own pulse and respiration.

His earpiece buzzed softly, and he was informed that the final defensive preparations were in place. With no further reason to delay, he nodded to the security chief and waited as she opened the airlock.

The heavy door swung open, and they peered into the darkness beyond. A glint of light reflected from a shiny surface that slowly resolved into the being that entered.

Two metres tall, the thing floated above the deck. The blue, metallic machine consisted of a central stalk that split at its top into three equally distributed necks. Each supported an eyeless, ellipsoidal head. Among them, the three heads commanded a full 360-degree view of its surroundings.

It advanced toward them, stopping a metre away. Shortly after, it was joined by two more of its kind. The normally roomy vestibule was uncomfortably cramped, but Hayden did not dare move lest any action be interpreted as hostile.

There was no way to tell if it had read or even seen Gabriel's board. The creatures gave no sign they recognized the presence of the humans. They remained motionless, seeming to wait for something.

Stella gasped. Terror contorted her face. Her eyes darted about, settling on Hayden, a pleading look in them. Before he could react, her eyelids snapped shut and she uttered guttural grunts.

Out of the corner of his eye, he spied movement. He shook his head at Atan, silently ordering her to stand down. The last thing he wanted to risk was anyone's actions being misinterpreted as aggressive.

Stella emitted awkward sounds that sounded like a baby discovering her voice. Gradually, grunts turned into tones that melodiously slid up and down her vocal range. Understandable, random words finally replaced the cacophony. Whispered at first, they became louder with each successive utterance, as if confidence was being built.

"Your species is unknown to us," said Stella, distantly.

Realizing the creatures were somehow speaking through her, Hayden said, "We are called human. We come from a system in one of the outer spiral arms of the galaxy." He hoped they had tapped into more than Stella's vocal control and would understand the meaning of his words.

"We are aware of yourself perception. This being has supplied what we require. Are you prepared for us to communicate through her?"

"We are." Hayden was torn between excitement at first contact and concern for what was happening to Stella. He prayed that his permitting her to join them had not doomed her to a horrible fate.

She suddenly relaxed and crumpled. Reflexively, he caught her. Cradled in his arms, she blinked several times before looking into his eyes.

"I... I'm all right. They want to use me as an interpreter. They say they are sorry for taking control of me against my will, but they had no other way to speak to us and had no way to confirm if we were sentient. They read my father's sign and took a chance."

Gabriel now knelt beside her as well, concern mixed with astonishment on his face. "Why did they select you?"

She closed her eyes, seeming to be listening to something. "They say they detected...I think they meant my feelings, but I'm not sure. I think they recognized my empathic ability and chose me."

"So, are they able to communicate with any of us in this manner?"

After another pause, she said, "Yes, a few of us. Most are blocked to them."

He considered that for a moment. "Do the LINK implants block them?"

"Yes, I think that's right."

She seized Hayden's sleeve, pulling him close. "They've seen what I've seen. They are aware of the Malliac. I think they want to help."

Council

ONE OF THE SENTINELS, as the creature had identified itself, led Hayden, Stella, and Gabriel into the hub. He'd ordered Atan to remain behind and keep an eye on the creatures that remained on the ship. It wasn't the Glenatat he mistrusted. He needed to make sure someone he trusted maintained discipline among the crew. The last thing he wanted was an incident that might jeopardize everyone.

"We are being taken to something they called the Council of Leaders," explained Stella. "These sentinels aren't alive."

"You mean they're artificial intelligences?"

"Not exactly. Our understanding of AI is very limited compared to them. They almost find the way we regard it insulting, if that is the right word."

"Please apologize for my ignorance," he said, quickly.

Stella smiled and placed a reassuring hand on his forearm. "Everything is okay, Hayden. They understand that no offence is intended."

"Are you able to talk without...?" He tipped his head slightly toward the sentinel that guided them through the complex.

"Yes, I can speak freely. They are not monitoring my thoughts anymore and only communicate through me with my permission. They were most apologetic for invading my mind. It is apparently a principle belief of theirs not to do so. They only resorted to it as a last act of desperation."

"How much do they know about us?"

"Everything; well, at least everything I know. They are eager to learn more about us."

Anticipation danced in Gabriel's eyes. "Are they willing to teach us about them?"

"That, I believe, is more difficult to answer. I think they may tell us what we are capable of understanding, though."

That was understandable to Hayden. How could an advanced, alien civilization be able to explain things beyond the human capacity to perceive? Everything humanity knew and believed it understood about the universe was filtered through senses and perceptions unique to life on Earth. Limited by biology, there were probably an infinite number of secrets humans would never be equipped to understand.

The sentinel led them to a circular doorway that irised open. They entered an expansive, dimly lit chamber.

"This is where we will meet the Council," said Stella, trepidation on her face, as if she had been shown something she dared not share.

Subdued blue lighting illuminated a large, cylindrical, aquarium-like structure in the centre of the room that rose from floor to a ceiling far above them. With every horror vid he ever watched foremost in his mind, Hayden tentatively advanced to the tank and peered through the transparent wall.

Suspended in a glowing, electric-blue fluid were five objects that resembled disembodied brains with four distinctive lobes. Hanging like a limp tail from each was what he assumed to be a vestigial spinal column.

"Are you the Glenatat?" asked Hayden.

After several seconds passed with no reply, he turned to Stella. "Can they hear me?"

"I don't know. I'm not getting anything from them now."

"But you recognize them, don't you?"

"Yes, but...no, I...think so. I don't know. I only saw a representation of them in my mind. I don't actually know what they look like."

He further scrutinized the beings. "Well, if not, then why the hell did they bring us here?"

As she struggled with an answer, his muscles stiffened, and his joints locked of their own accord.

"Hayden, what's the matter?"

"I hear...something."

"Voices?"

He nodded.

Her hand gently grasped his forearm. "I do too. We're not hearing them with our ears. That's how they communicate: by stimulating the auditory cortex of the brain."

Regaining control of his body, he peered at the creatures in the tank. "Do I speak my reply, or will they read my thoughts?"

"Just talk with them as if you had your LINK. I can hear you both."

Hayden focused his attention on the aliens. His forehead creased in concentration as he considered the closest one.

Hello? Can you understand me?

We do.

The reply seemed to come from nowhere.

He made another tentative search of the room before turning back to them. *With which one of you do I communicate?*

A long pause followed. He turned to Stella and her father, puzzled.

"What's wrong?" asked Gabriel.

"I think I maybe insulted them."

You have caused no offence. We are one.

He spun about. "You can hear what I say?"

We perceive the intent of your communication as you formulate it.

"So, I only need to speak?"

You experience less distress to do so.

He grinned, but it faded quickly when he realized he was the only one who heard them.

"My companion informs me that you want to help us," he said to them.

Your vessel, and some of you are damaged. We will repair you.

"We are grateful for your generosity."

We have identified several habitable worlds suited to your species, once your repairs are completed.

"Um, with apologies, but we wish to return to our home world."

One of the disembodied brains pulsed like a swimming jellyfish. In turn, each of the remaining ones alternately mimicked the action. Hayden turned to Stella, an unspoken question on his face.

"Perhaps they're discussing your request?" she posited.

As if responding to Stella's speculation, the Glenatat voice rang once more in his head.

Your vessel and your damaged companions will be repaired, but we will not return you to your world. You will be accommodated on a terrestrial planet within the protected dimensional matrix.

"I don't understand what that is."

It is a transdimensional construct that permits multiple planets to occupy the interior of the defensive structure surrounding this star system.

"How many worlds are you talking about?"

One hundred and ninety-four thousand are under our protection.

Hayden's mouth dropped open. "How is that even possible?"

The explanation is beyond your species' limited capacity to comprehend.

Mildly insulted, Hayden asked, "What did you mean when you said they are protected?"

We defend a multitude of civilizations under threat from the Dark Malice; those you refer to as Malliac.

Suddenly the great scorch marks on the surface of the Dyson sphere made sense.

"Who or what are they?"

Another long pause ensued while the Glenatat conferred.

Forgive our delay, but it was necessary to access your ship's complete knowledge base to provide you with an answer appropriate to your technological development. The Malliac are demons.

"What? There are no such things. They are living creatures. We've killed them. They are a dark matter life form."

Their nature is beyond your species' limited capacity to comprehend.

Hayden frowned. The last thing he wanted to do was antagonize their hosts. This was annoyingly like some of the diplomatic exercises at the academy. At the time, he hadn't the patience for what he considered unlikely scenarios contrived by his instructors. He realized that he owed them an apology.

Softening his facial expression, he smiled and said, "We are a curious race, eager to learn. Would you indulge our curiosity about them?"

Yet again the Glenatat conferred among themselves.

The substance you call dark matter threads through subdimensional space and time. It is where the Malliac were formed. Eons ago, they emerged to savage our empire. They spread, consuming the resources of star systems they encounter.

"What do they want?"

Their purpose is to survive.

"They sound like a plague of locusts," Hayden muttered.

We built this fortress to collect and preserve the civilized planets of our dominion that were endangered by them.

"How long ago did these events happen?"

By your measurement of time, nine hundred thousand of your years.

"They have been spreading out across the galaxy since that time?"

They advance slowly, constrained by the physical laws of this dimension, exhausting their resources as they do so. Their number decreases as they travel between systems that can support them. Our projections show they will become extinct within half a galactic rotation.

"They invaded our Mu Arae colony, with millions of people. Everything was destroyed."

The Glenatat pulsed in their tank. *We were not aware of your species, nor that you occupied a system we abandoned. We grieve with you.*

"How far have they advanced since your encounter with them?"

An image of the galaxy flashed in his mind, showing the historic advance of the Malliac. After studying the map, he said, "This indicates they are moving farther into our region of space."

It is their nature.

"How can they be stopped?"

There is no means.

"We destroyed two of their ships before our arrival here."

You overcame isolated representatives of their species. When they descend upon a star system, they do so en masse, bringing all their destructive power to the task.

"Is that what happened to the planet Dulcinea...the world you abandoned?"

Yes.

"Why do they destroy worlds instead of occupy them?" asked Stella. Perspiration glistened on her forehead and Hayden suddenly realized how his emotional reaction to what he heard must be affecting her.

They harvest the latent energy within the cores of terrestrial planets. Once satiated, they move on to other star systems.

"How did you overcome them?"

We did not. They will cease to exist when the resources available to them become exhausted as they advance to the outer rim, where stars are fewer and more widely distributed.

"We live in that region of the galaxy. Trillions of my people are in the path of those creatures. Surely you possess the means to help us defend ourselves against them. You successfully held them at bay with this fortress."

Your species is not significant.

Tears were in Stella's eyes. "So, you're just going to let them destroy us?"

It is unavoidable. They will eventually expire. There is no logic for us to expend resources to accomplish what nature will over time.

"It won't happen before they overrun us," said Hayden.

You have many centuries to escape the advancing Malliac.

"With all due respect, if you return us to our home, we can warn our people now."

That is not possible. We will provide you aid and sanctuary, but you will not be permitted to leave this place.

Making a Plan

HAYDEN SAT, SQUEEZED between Stella and Cora, in the captain's quarters, where Pavlovich had decided to hold the debriefing.

"A fat lot of good your diplomatic skills did us, Kaine. We're marooned."

"With respect, sir, I..."

The captain waved his hand dismissively. "I know, I know. You steered the crippled ship into a safe port and persuaded the natives to welcome us and nurse our wounds. That was your first responsibility. For what it's worth, you did good, and I suppose I'll have to commend you in my log."

"Thank you, sir..."

"The ironic part of it all is that you did better at commanding than at the diplomatic thing you want to spend the rest of your career doing."

"Captain," said Stella, "We might find ourselves adrift again, if forced to rely on your diplomacy skills."

Pavlovich scowled at her. "Why, exactly, are you here?"

Hayden cleared his throat. "She's here at my invitation, sir. I believe her initial connection to the Glenatat provides us with the best insight into our hosts."

The captain grunted. "How much did you learn, Miss Gabriel?"

"What I saw was almost overwhelming," she said. "They are, as my father has said, an ancient race whose empire once spread across a quarter of the galaxy. Those forms we saw in the chamber—"

"The brains in the tank that Kaine described?"

"Yes. They are vestigial structures that they occupy when communicating with less evolved species."

"You mean they wear them like a formal uniform or something?"

"Yes, I think so. Most of their time is spent elsewhere...a different dimension, I guess we'd call it."

"So, the gods spend their time on Olympus, or Valhalla or wherever, and condescend to take on corporeal form to commune with us mere mortals?"

"Captain! That really isn't what I meant."

"I'm sorry. I suppose I should show more gratitude toward them for fixing my damaged brain."

"We should be grateful they chose to give us aid," she said.

"You don't think they are disposed to charity to strangers?"

"Quite the contrary, Captain, I got the sense that they are xenophobic in the extreme."

"They made it clear that our species wasn't worth saving. Why are they helping us at all?" asked Hayden.

"Curiosity, I think," she said. "I was exposed to a lot on our first connection before they cut me off. They seemed almost desperate to discover everything I knew about the Malliac."

"Did you get any indication from them for the reason they don't want us to leave?"

"No, but one thing became clear during our meeting with them. They are afraid."

"You got that through your own abilities?"

She nodded. "They couldn't hide their fear. The Glenatat seemed genuinely relieved that the Malliac are moving into our part of the galaxy."

"Well," said Pavlovich, "if they're scared, it might be something we can use to our advantage."

"How so, sir?" asked Hayden.

"If they believe the Malliac have our scent and will follow us here, maybe they'll be more inclined to send us on our way."

"Or simply destroy us."

Hayden turned to Stella. "Did you get a sense that was a possibility during your connection?"

"I... I don't think so. They seemed benevolent."

Pavlovich shook his head. "I think if they wanted us dead, we would be by now. They didn't seem to mind lending Cora a pet to help her fix the ship."

"He has been very helpful, Cap'n," she said, "and he would be insulted to hear you call him that."

"You didn't have to name the thing."

"Well, he didn't have one, and I couldn't keep saying, 'Hey you,' so he agreed to me calling him Alcon."

"I see." Hayden tried hide his growing smile.

"Speaking of your new toy," said Pavlovich, "is everything back online?"

"Oh, we finished that an hour ago. Alcon was very helpful; taught me a few new tricks. We've increased the efficiency of our engines by forty percent." She grinned. "He's updating our navigational charts for this sector."

"It didn't happen to tell you how we can get home using them?" asked the captain.

Her smile wavered. "Sorry, Cap'n."

"Hmph."

"How are you feeling, sir?" asked Hayden.

"Why? Are you tired of command already, Kaine?"

"No, sir—I mean—"

"Relax, Lieutenant. Her damned pet is a better med than our synths. It repaired everyone who was injured."

The room became quiet.

He shrugged. "The doc still wants me under observation for a couple of days, so you still technically are in command. Try not to pooch things up."

"Yes, sir."

Another awkward silence filled the room.

Pavlovich said, "So, what is your plan...Captain?"

"Well, I'm not content to accept the decision to keep us here. If they are afraid of the Malliac, as Stella suspects, there may be an opportunity to play on that fear."

"Even if you can persuade them to let us go, there is still the problem of finding our way back to our part of the galaxy," said Cora.

"With the updated charts, we can probably navigate our way to the wormhole that brought us here."

"That plan will land us back in a nest full of Malliac and no closer to home," said Pavlovich.

"Then I'll come up with a reason for them to send us back to Earth, or at least upgrade our weaponry," said Hayden. "Surely the Glenatat have something more sophisticated than our rail guns."

"Don't let Gunney hear you say that," Cora said, smiling.

"As of this moment, our top priority is to find a way home. Our duty is to warn the Confederation about the Malliac before they invade another of our systems. The only way we are going to do that is with Glenatat help. Your work is cut out for you, Captain Kaine."

Doubts

"WHAT'S WRONG, HAYDEN?"

The meeting over, Stella and Hayden left Pavlovich's quarters. As they walked the corridor in silence, he felt her eyes on him.

"It's nothing."

She touched his arm, and they stopped walking. "What is it?"

"Just something the captain said, about my diplomacy..."

"He's a grumpy old man who has a great deal on his mind. I'm sure he didn't mean anything by it. You're the only person who could speak for us, and I think you did a marvellous job."

"Thanks, but it got me thinking. The diplomatic corps was to be my ticket to political office, but that was in a world without the Malliac or the Glenatat. With this new danger brewing, relations between squabbling planetary governments may be the least of humankind's worries."

He looked into her eyes and blushed. "I'm sorry. I'm self-absorbed, worrying about my career path when everyone's life here is uncertain."

"You are, but the fact that you are bothered by what my opinion is says a lot for your progress." She stood on her toes and kissed him on the cheek. "You succeeded in getting a group of xenophobic aliens to take us in, patch up our wounds, and offer us sanctuary. That's pretty good for a neophyte captain or diplomat, in my books. I suspect your career prospects are still good."

He smiled and squeezed her hand. "I suppose I should focus on the task of getting us back to our part of the galaxy."

"You are on your shift break. You should get some rest." She wrapped her arms about his waist and pulled him close. "Besides, is there a rush to get started on sweet-talking the Glenatat?"

"Well, no. Not if you can think of a better idea."

With a sly smile, she disengaged herself and led him by the hand to her quarters.

A few hours later, they lay entangled in the sheets together. Stella snored softly while Hayden gently caressed her bare shoulder.

She stirred. He hugged her warm body to him.

"What time is it?" she asked.

He checked his chronometer. A "watch" was what Pavlovich called the antique when he gave it to him.

"This isn't a gift, Kaine." the captain had told him. "With your LINK out of commission, I don't want any excuses for you being late."

"It's 0300," Hayden told Stella. "I'm not on duty for another three hours."

"Mm," she purred as she snuggled into him.

Stella shot upright; her eyes wide. He was about to ask her what was wrong when he heard the voice inside his head too.

The Glenatat had summoned them both.

A Change of Heart

HAYDEN AND STELLA STOOD before the tank. Joining them was Ishmael Gabriel.

The Glenatat had granted the scientist's request for the sentinel to remove his LINK so he could communicate with them. Pavlovich agreed to the procedure, but the man's presence at this meeting still irritated Hayden.

"You're letting us return home?" he said to the creatures. "What changed your minds?"

Our sentinel's analysis of your ship's jump engines revealed a danger that must be addressed.

Hayden's mouth went dry. His concern grew that a tactical blunder was made in permitting Cora to give Alcon free access to their systems. Though the decision was made by Pavlovich while Hayden was occupied elsewhere, whatever happened while he was still in command was his responsibility. The fact that the captain momentarily forgot his place when he gave permission would be immaterial at Kaine's court martial.

"What has your analysis revealed?"

While your understanding of the physics of transdimensional transport is primitive, the technique employed by you is innovative.

Confused by the compliment, he replied, "Thank you. Our ship's design is not a current example of..."

The manner by which you generate a stable portal is elegant and simple, and therein lies a danger.

"What is it?"

The Malliac have the technical ability to exploit a flaw in your technology. They will soon gain access to your transdimensional network.

"How is that possible? Our jump-gates have been secure for almost three centuries."

The mathematics is beyond—

187

"Is beyond my species' capacity to understand. Yes, I know. Would you please indulge me?"

He felt Stella's hand on his arm and glanced to her. Her eyes warned him to be cautious.

Your engines are designed to use a captured singularity to facilitate transit across the transdimensional barrier.

"Yes, each engine is coded with a specifically balanced artificial micro-black hole, tuned to the mass and quantum sum of the ship."

As said, the method is primitive. The nature of your gate design makes it vulnerable to a forced breach if an assemblage of singularities is employed.

Hayden racked his brain, attempting to recall his transdimensional physics. "A tuned array of that proportion should be physically impossible to control."

Using your species' primitive understanding of mathematics, that is a reasonable assumption.

"Of course!" Gabriel smacked his forehead with his palm.

"Doctor?"

"I didn't take into account the Hancock variables, because they don't apply to normal matter."

"What are you talking about?"

"I'm afraid I wasn't entirely truthful with you about why I was harvesting singularities. I am aware of this vulnerability. I was working on a means to create a modified tuned assembly of them to facilitate our escape from Mu Arae. I abandoned the work when I encountered a problem in my equations."

"I don't understand."

"Isn't it obvious? The mathematics only applies to dark matter. In fact, everything is much simpler."

"You mean they are telling the truth? The Malliac can hack our jump-gates?"

"Yes, they can use their assemblage of singularities as a substitute portal to move directly into transdimensional space."

"How many would they need?"

Gabriel shook his head with a helpless expression. "To answer that I need to know the combined dark-mass equivalent they intend to transport."

"Shit!" Turning his attention back to the Glenatat, Hayden said, "What can be done to prevent them from doing this?"

Preventing it is not possible. We will send you back to your domain. You must warn your people of the danger that is upon them.

"But you said yourself, there is no way to stop them when they attack as a collective."

There is no way to resist their onslaught. There is only escape.

"What the hell has changed your minds? When did we become important enough for you to care what happens to us?"

The hum of the machines that maintained the tank was their only reply. Hayden stared at the floor, trying to take it all in.

"Can you do anything to rescue any of the worlds in immediate danger? You managed to save thousands of your own threatened planets."

There is insufficient capacity to accommodate all the systems now under threat. With access to transdimensional space, the Malliac will not diminish, but flourish. Within five hundred thousand of your years they will overrun the galaxy.

"So you're just going to throw every civilization out there to those monsters until only you survive in your perfect little protected bubble. What will you do when they finally come for you?"

Stella's hand again grasped his arm, but he shook her off and shouted at them. "You are a band of cowards."

Your species need not perish. Warned, many can flee the onslaught.

"And become a hunted diaspora, forever running."

Only until your natural extinction takes place.

"Then why bother with us at all?"

The Malliac are only interested in resources. Our projections suggest that there is a small probability you can evolve into something significant. We must preserve that possible outcome, no matter how small.

"Tell that to those of my crew who they killed. We've seen first-hand the level of disinterest they show my kind."

We will transport your ship to your home system, where you can warn your people. We regret there is little else we can do.

Abruptly, the lights in the tank went out and the Glenatat brain structures stopped moving.

"I guess the interview is over."

Stella approached him and wrapped her arms around him. "I know you feel bad, but none of this is your fault."

He broke the embrace. "Why do I feel that there is more I could do? They are washing their hands of any involvement."

"They can't be shamed by you, Mister Kaine," said Gabriel. "What you see as a moral responsibility is a foreign concept to them. Their only interest is in preserving the possibility that we might one day become a peer to them."

"I know. I just feel helpless. If we knew about all this when we arrived at Mu Arae, we could have destroyed the jump-gate."

"Oh, you wouldn't want to do that. It would be almost as disastrous as permitting the Malliac to exploit it."

"How is that?"

"Well, the only way to destroy it is to sever its link with transdimensional space. One would have to remove the gateway itself from our space-time. Doing so would theoretically loop the connecting string structures back on themselves."

"Would dropping it into a black hole accomplish the same thing?"

"In theory, it is possible. But you would never want to do that."

"Why not, if it could prevent the Malliac from accessing it?"

"Because in the act of destroying it, you would collapse the entire network as well. You would effectively destroy the means of travel between connected star systems. It would isolate every world within the confederacy."

Hayden furrowed his brow as he considered what he just heard.

Stella watched him with concern. "What are you thinking?"

"There may be a way to stop them."

A Call to Arms

THE IMPATIENT CREW was gathered in the mess hall for the arrival of Captain Pavlovich. Rumours ran through the ship like a wildfire, and everyone anticipated an announcement about their return home.

People's disposition toward Hayden had been mollified considerably. They now greeted him with a friendly smile or a nod, rather than sullen deference to the man they held responsible for their situation. With the prospect of returning to Earth at hand, his brief time as captain was regarded in a new, favourable light.

He sat in the first row, staring at the deck and wringing his sweaty hands. Stella was beside him, seemingly basking in the collective feelings of happy anticipation.

On his other side was Cora. With all systems running like new, she was the picture of contentment. As the freshly appointed chief engineer, she was aware of the proposed plan. If she had reservations about it, she kept them to herself.

"Aten-hut!" called Atan, who stood rigidly at attention near the hatchway. As Pavlovich entered, the crew rose to their feet and offered him enthusiastic applause.

Taking his position at the front of the room, he waved for silence. "At ease. Sit down and relax, people. I didn't exactly come back from the dead."

After everyone settled into their chairs, he took stock of the room. Beneath his black beard the hint of a smile grew. "First, I want to commend your XO for his exemplary performance as acting captain. You saved all our asses, Lieutenant. There will be a commendation on your record when we return home." He looked down at his notes and swallowed hard.

"Since it is impossible to keep anything secret on this ship, you are all aware, the Glenatat offered to send us back to Earth—"

A round of applause rose up. Pavlovich grimaced and allowed the noise to die down. "What you do not know are the circumstances behind this offer."

He went on to outline the situation and the danger to the Confederacy.

"They are giving us the opportunity to sound the warning bell, but the event it forewarns will be catastrophic for humanity."

The room was deathly quiet. Pavlovich dispassionately described the outcome of a Malliac invasion of human space.

"Now, I don't think anyone in this room relishes us being the harbingers of apocalyptic news. If I had even the smallest chance to stop the bastards, I would sooner die in the attempt than run from them in shame for the rest of my life."

A few people shouted assent, and some small pockets of short-lived clapping erupted.

"Some of you may not feel the way I do. God knows we've paid a dear price with our own blood by taking on the Malliac. But this is a warship of the Confederation. We aren't the most up-to-date ship in the fleet, and Central Command doesn't hold some of this crew in high regard..." He stole a glance at Hayden and winked. "But we are all blooded warriors! We each took an oath to fight for, and if necessary, die to protect the empire. I think if it were possible, every one of you would honour your promise without hesitation."

The room erupted in cheers as people rose to their feet to affirm Pavlovich's words. Hayden wondered how their enthusiasm would hold up when they learned the plan.

"Well, as it happens, there is such an opportunity. I won't sugarcoat things. This is risky, and many of us will not survive. While the price to be paid is dear, if we succeed, our loved ones and every citizen of the Confederacy will sleep soundly in their own bed at night and not run fleeing before the alien threat."

He briefly outlined their plan. Hayden looked behind him. Faces were grim, and jaws clenched tight as the captain described the risks.

"If we do this, and succeed, the Malliac advance across the galaxy will be checked at Mu Arae. They won't be a danger to anyone for at least another decade. Forewarned, with enough time, humanity will prepare for their eventual arrival. Now that we know what they are, there is a fighting chance to save our homes.

"But the cost of this opportunity will be great. There will no longer be a United Confederation of Planets. All the colony worlds will become isolated. The only means of transit between them will be at subluminal velocity. We will be making the decision to cast humanity's capacity for interstellar travel back by three hundred years. And we will be cursed for it. There is no doubt about that."

Deathly silence filled the hall. Hayden glanced at Stella. Tears ran down her cheeks as she suffered the confusion and anguish of every person in the room.

"I understand if there are some of you who may not wish to take part in what we must do. Had we the time, I would take this proposal to the High Command, but we don't. Every minute we discuss and debate the ethics and morality of this plan, the creatures draw closer to breaking through. Hell, for all we know, they already have, and we are too late."

Stella's fingers dug into Hayden's knee, and she winced.

"What's wrong?" he asked.

"Just a lot of strong emotions. I'll be fine."

Pavlovich continued. "I will not order you to participate in this mission. You all will have to examine your conscience and decide for yourself. I won't look unkindly on a person who objects to this action on moral or personal grounds. We've advised our hosts of our intentions, and the cowardly bastards agreed to let us take it on the chin for them. They will transport those who don't want to join us back to your home world. You can be with your families and live a life, safe from the Malliac. I won't think poorly of anyone who makes that choice. After that, they intend to shut down their own network to isolate themselves."

"For those of you who come with me, the Glenatat will send us back to Mu Arae. There, our mission will be to destroy the jump-gate and end the immediate threat."

Hayden found himself on his feet. "Count me in, Captain."

Soon he was followed by one, then three, then the rest of the crew. All pledged their lives to the cause. He glanced at Stella, still sitting, who looked up at him with tear-filled eyes. She grasped his hand and shook her head before she also stood.

"You and your father can return to Earth or wherever you want."

She sniffed. "I know. But my ability is something you will need if you are going to pull this off. And besides, I don't want to be apart from you." She kissed him on the cheek.

He squeezed her hand and reluctantly joined in with the cheering.

Scimitar was going to war.

Temptation

RETREATING TO HIS CABIN, Hayden collapsed on the bunk.

As much as he wanted Stella to join him, he was glad she decided to spend the last few hours with her father. It was a wise move, since they would never see each other again. Gabriel intended to remain with the Glenatat. The odds were overwhelming that none of them would survive.

The other reason he didn't want her present was a selfish one.

Immediately after his declaration of support for the mission, the consequences of his impetuous act flooded his mind and threatened to overwhelm him.

He thought he did an admirable job of holding himself together while she was with him; he didn't believe she detected the conflicting emotions he fought to control. If she had, she graciously ignored them, allowing him his privacy.

What had he done?

He should be opting for the safe thing: hop on one of the transport pods going home. Whether *Scimitar* was successful or not, people with first-hand experience of the Malliac would be needed to lead the defence against their eventual arrival.

Even if Pavlovich beat the odds and succeeded in destroying the jump-gate, an isolated Sol would still be the most populated system in the galaxy. The one hundred billion people there would need real leadership, individuals who could take up the torch and lead them through the dark times of rebuilding. As a returning hero, his election to the council would be all but guaranteed. Everything he was meant to be was within his grasp, in one swooping action.

Success or failure of the mission, his fate on Earth was a better one than if he remained on *Scimitar*.

What had he been thinking when he opened his big mouth?

He didn't think, that was the problem.

The captain's words had stunned the crew into silence. Nobody was going to be the first to volunteer, so he jumped up first, without thought. Caught up in his role as first officer, he had acted without considering the personal cost.

He chuckled. What would his father say if he were here?

Would he be praised as a leader or berated for throwing away a chance to fulfill his destiny? Probably the latter, he decided.

The plotting and planning of three generations of Kaines was now a pile of smouldering ash. He would die at the farthest reaches of the empire, and nobody would know. Everything he was meant to be, all that he had been pushed to become, was now moot.

Hayden never considered the idea his life might end up any other way. He took everything for granted, scoffed at it, and petulantly acted out against it, knowing in the back of his mind that he would eventually arrive wherever his family had steered him.

Had he volunteered to spite them? He didn't know.

All he knew was that his feet were now firmly set upon a path he never intended to take.

His life was over; he was dead, even before the battle.

He was unable to hold back tears any longer.

He didn't even know who he wept for.

Hayden's Choice

HAYDEN SAT ON THE END of his bed, head in his hands, when the door buzzer roused him from his thoughts.

"Come in."

He looked up at Stella, standing in the doorway, concern etched on her face.

"What's wrong?"

Inhaling deeply, he stretched his arms over his head. "Nothing. I was just reflecting on what we're about to attempt."

As he stood, a holo-photo fell from his lap to the floor. She picked it up. The picture was of a young boy and a man, laughing and enjoying a day of fishing.

"Is this your father?"

He joined her in examining it. "I was eight. He thought it was time I learned how to fish. I don't know why it was so vital to him that I learn. He never fished, and we never did it again. I think it was traditional; his father did the same with him."

She handed it back to him. "Is tradition important in your family?"

He guffawed. "It *is* family, as far as Dad is concerned."

"I don't understand."

"Every Kaine has their life planned and mapped out. There is a predefined purpose for each of us. It probably begins at birth, but it wouldn't surprise me to learn that he has plans for any children I sire."

"And what is your intended destiny?"

"I was supposed to be the first of my family to achieve the presidency of the Confederation."

Stella's eyebrows rose. "Really?"

"Yeah. It sounds arrogant, doesn't it?"

"Maybe a little presumptuous; prematurely optimistic, perhaps. Possibly..."

"Delusional?"

199

"I wasn't going to say that."

"That's how I've referred to it in the past. I am deluded. Now it is about to become impossible."

"You're disappointed."

"It would be foolish of me to deny that to you." He smiled.

She took his hand and sat beside him.

He said, "For my entire life, everything I did, every school I attended or friendship I cultivated, was for a purpose. My life path was plainly laid out. I was to complete my academy training, serve in some safe posting in the diplomatic corps, and then graduate into politics with a respectable military career behind me. Being posted in space, becoming a fleet officer, going to war—none of it was in the plan."

"I don't know too many people who live their lives according to a schedule."

"You haven't met my family. My grandfather plotted Dad's life with the goal to get me into the academy. This objective has been my family's sole focus for four generations."

"That's a heavy burden to carry," she said.

"Yeah, especially when everything is about to blow up. I'm facing choices that nobody ever dreamed of."

"But that's the way life works, Hayden."

"Not for the Kaines."

"You're afraid you're going to be a disappointment to your father?"

"Hell, no. I already did that. But there was always the chance that I could fight my way back; redeem myself."

"And now?"

"Now I'm about to partake in a mission that will destroy the empire they wanted me to govern."

"But it's for the greater good. You said so yourself."

"Yes, the alternative of billions of deaths and an unwinnable conflict is far worse."

"But...?"

He looked into her questioning eyes, searching for a safe place to land. "I can't help but think there is a way for me to salvage something of the family plan. I could take the Glenatat offer and return to Earth. Even cut off from the rest of the Confederacy, there will be the opportunity to work myself into a political career path."

"You want to please your father, don't you?"

He looked at the photo, still in his hand. "I don't think that's possible. This is one of the few times I recall him being happy or seeming to be."

"Then what do you want?"

"I want the guilt to go away. If we succeed, we will become the most vilified group in human history. Destroying the jump network will alter humankind's destiny. Nobody will remember that we saved them from an overwhelming threat. We're the only ones who've seen them. The Malliac will only be an idea to everyone else."

"Well, you have a decision to make. The plan can be carried out without you. You can work your way to the presidency and salvage your family's dream. You might even be able to repatriate everyone's reputation."

"Are you saying I should go?"

She held his hand. "I'm telling you to go where your conscience tells you to. I won't think poorly of you if you return to Earth."

"You wouldn't come with me?"

Stella shook her head, sadness in her eyes. "No, my love, I know what my destiny is; what my gift is meant for. I cannot go with you."

"I can't begin to imagine what Pavlovich would say. I was the first to jump up and support him."

"Why does his opinion matter? Or mine? The Hayden Kaine I first met didn't care about any of that sort of affirmation. Your goal has always been to get back to your old life—your real life, as you call it."

"That was..."

The mirror Stella held up for him hid nothing and starkly showed him what she saw. A self-absorbed jerk. He didn't need her empathic ability to see she was hurt and disappointed by him.

What had changed? A few short weeks ago, he would happily have hitched a ride back to Earth without giving *Scimitar* or anyone here a second thought. Returning would not be an act of cowardice. It would be patriotic; loyal. Faithful to his father's dream.

He looked into Stella's eyes. Instead of resentment or anger, he saw only compassion.

It had never really been his ambition. He realized that he never truly had one of his own, until now. Looking at her, he understood where his place was and what he must do.

"My life is here. My destiny hasn't been written."

Going Back

THE BRIDGE WAS ABUZZ with preparations to depart the Glenatat protective sphere. Pavlovich ruled over it all from his command chair. He was no micromanager. He trusted his people to perform their duties without unnecessary nagging. His imposing presence was intimidating enough. Hayden realized it was one of the things that endeared the big man to him.

"Mister Kaine, what is the status of our modifications?"

"Main engines are upgraded as per the new specs. Our top subluminal speed is 0.9c. Corresponding inertial compensation fields are integrated into our gravity plating."

"What about the weapons?"

Hayden glanced to Gunney's empty alcove. "Dark energy cannons are installed and complement our rail gun arrays. The hull is reinforced with a layer of the material that composes the Dyson sphere. Our sensors are enhanced to detect dark matter."

"So, we'll be able to see the bastards coming? Good. Anything else?"

"The Glenatat provided us with one of their sentinels to assist with tactical analysis and emergency repairs. I stationed it in engineering."

"Cora will be happy to have her pet again."

The captain made an admiring survey of his bridge crew then picked up a data pad and handed it to Hayden. "Take a look at that, Kaine. Not a single person wanted to return home. We had to draw lots to select who would go to the key systems and inform them of what is going on. We don't want to turn out the lights without giving them an explanation of why it happened."

Hayden swallowed the lump in his throat and returned the pad to Pavlovich. "They are an admirable crew, sir. You should be pleased."

"I'm very proud of this bunch. But you, Kaine, surprised me. I've never had an XO whom I can say was worthy of the position, until now."

"Thank you, Captain. It has been an honour to serve with you." Surprising himself, he realized he meant every word.

The hatch swung open, and the gunnery officer clanked his way into the bridge. He nodded to Hayden and Pavlovich and took his place in his alcove.

"What do you think of your new arsenal, Gunney?" asked the captain.

The cyborg grunted. "It all sounds impressive until something fails. The rail guns are all up to spec. I have no doubts about them, but these new weapons... I'll want to run a full test of 'em before I'm satisfied."

"I'm sure we can find an asteroid or two for you to shoot at." The captain lowered his voice and addressed Hayden. "What about your girlfriend? Is she up for the task, or do I need to leave her here with her father?"

"Stella is ready."

Cora entered the bridge and assumed her place at the engineering station.

"Well, Chief Engineer?" asked Pavlovich. "How is my ship?"

"*Scimitar* hasn't been this good since she came off the assembly line, Cap'n."

"Any problem with the Glenatat modifications?"

"Not one, sir. Alcon has done a great job of integrating our technologies."

"Don't get too attached to that thing, Cora. It is not one of the crew, and I won't treat it as one."

"No need to worry. I'll keep him out of your beard. You won't even know he's aboard."

"Make sure of that." Pavlovich looked about the bridge. "It's time, Mister Kaine."

"Aye-aye, sir."

Hayden gave the order to release the mooring clamps. A Glenatat vessel waiting nearby remotely took control of the helm to escort them out.

"No tractor beams this time, Ensign Kwok. Be prepared to take over after we clear the entrance," said Kaine.

Scimitar, as if on its own, followed the alien ship through the opening and into the larger Dyson sphere. The bright red sun, millions of kilometres away at the centre of the enormous structure, shone brightly, bathing everything in a gentle, ruddy glow.

"I find it almost unimaginable that a race capable of this kind of engineering miracle found themselves helpless against the Malliac," said Pavlovich. "There is no way humanity would survive an encounter with them. We are doing the right thing."

Assuming we can succeed, thought Hayden. Their plan to destroy the jump-gate and collapse the transdimensional network was almost impossible. In the hundreds of simulations he ran, only a fraction of the scenarios resulted in a successful completion of the mission. Most of the runs predicted *Scimitar's* failure and destruction. The chances of success were ridiculously tiny. This was shaping up to be a one-way trip, no matter how he looked at it; if they failed, he would die. If they succeeded, he could still perish. His career plans and his future would be gone. Everyone who survived the ordeal would be marooned forever in the Mu Arae system.

He regretted his decision, not sure being a hero was worth the price asked of him.

The hatchway opened, and Stella stepped into the bridge. Pavlovich glanced in her direction and acknowledged her with a curt nod. She saw Hayden and smiled at him from across the room. His mouth curled upward, and his gaze lingered.

He didn't know from where she got her courage. She had survived all those years, running from an invisible enemy, growing up isolated from society. How could she turn out to have her shit together better than he?

Their lives couldn't be more different. He was raised in the lap of privilege. With every advantage going for him, he ended up as an arrogant, self-absorbed asshole who believed the universe owed him a guaranteed future. And yet, despite all his shortcomings, she seemed to genuinely care for him.

He turned from her and pretended to examine the readout at his station. A moment later, he felt her warmth as she sidled up and peeked over his shoulder at what commanded his attention.

Switching the display off, he faced her. "How is the crew holding up?"

"Difficult to tell when they are all experiencing the same thing. Anxious and maybe a little excited. How are you feeling?"

"You can't tell?"

"I'm trying not to read you—it's challenging."

He lowered his voice. "It would be a lie if I told you I didn't have doubts." He discreetly intertwined his fingers with hers. "I'm okay and ready to see this thing through."

She raised a questioning eyebrow before standing on her toes and kissing him on the cheek.

"I am assigned to Medical until you need me. I just came up to say good luck."

He squeezed her hand and then watched as she departed the bridge.

"A good companion in life can give us the strength we otherwise lack, Kaine," Pavlovich said quietly.

Hayden felt his face grow warm. "Have you ever had anyone like that in your life, Captain?"

Pavlovich raised his hands to indicate the surroundings. "*Scimitar*. She has yet to fail me and never ceases to astound me with her strength."

Hayden smiled. "I meant a person, sir."

"A long time ago." The captain placed a large, meaty hand on Hayden's shoulder. "She's a good one, Kaine. Remember that."

The next half hour passed in relative silence as *Scimitar* journeyed through the Dyson sphere.

When the ship exited the structure, their escort relinquished control of the helm. As the vessel departed, the Glenatat spoke to Hayden one final time.

Farewell, and may your mission find success.

Reflexively, he glanced about to see if anyone else had heard the message, but everyone seemed preoccupied with their assigned tasks.

It was all well and good for their hosts to arm *Scimitar* and send her off to her likely doom. He didn't understand how such a powerful race could be so ambivalent about the fate of the rest of the galaxy.

From his diplomacy training, he understood that negotiation always revolved around a common understanding or value. He had no clue what the Glenatat valued. Did they simply view humanity as a blunt instrument to take care of their problem?

As he reflected, he realized that their approach was not dissimilar to how he had used those around him to his ends.

Perhaps he had more in common with them than he wanted to admit.

Flexing Their Muscles

"REPORT," SAID PAVLOVICH. "Get me a location fix. Where are we?"

His call to routine snapped the bridge crew out of their torpor. Hayden shook his head to clear away the disorientating effects of the passage through the wormhole. A glance at the captain, who massaged his temples with both hands, confirmed that he too had been affected.

Suddenly recalling the Malliac, he rushed to the science station and initiated a scan with their enhanced instruments.

"I have a star chart match," said Kwok. "We are 70,000 kilometres from our last recorded position in the Mu Arae system."

"Practically a bull's-eye," muttered Pavlovich. "Are the bugs deployed yet?"

"They're working, Captain," Hayden said. "Initial midrange scans show no Malliac engine signatures in the area, sir." He attempted to hide the relief in his voice.

"I thought you reported two of their ships destroyed by us near here?"

Frowning, Hayden returned his attention to the instruments. "That's correct, Captain."

"Well, there should be some wreckage, shouldn't there?"

"It's possible their inertia carried—wait, I found something."

He felt every eye on him while he adjusted the readout.

"I can't understand the data on the Glenatat dark matter band, but we're picking up something odd on conventional scans."

"I need something actionable, Kaine," said Pavlovich, scowling.

"This is weird. I'm getting fluctuating graviton emissions. I can't get a fix on the mass of whatever it is."

"Cora," growled the captain, "I thought you told me our instruments were up to snuff."

"They are, Cap'n," she said. "I tested them myself."

She moved to the science station and took over the analysis. After a few tense minutes, she said, "Everything is working perfectly, sir."

"Then how do you explain the gravity anomalies?"

"Whatever that thing is, its mass is flickering on and off, like it can't decide if it exists or not."

"Cora, that's impossible," said Hayden.

"Yeah, I know, relativity and all that. But that is what the instruments tell me, and I believe them."

"Can you give me a visual?"

Cora's hands played over the terminal and the image on the forward viewer switched to a familiar field of stars. In the middle of the hologram drifted something Hayden had seen once before. "It's a Malliac ship," he said. "It looks dead."

Every part of it seemed to flicker in and out of existence as the hulk floated, like a ghost.

"What the hell?" said Pavlovich. "Gunney!"

"It's in my sights, sir. All weapons are hot and at your command."

"Gimme a second, Cap'n," said Cora as she returned to her engineering station. "I'm going to patch Alcon into the feed."

The captain shot her a withering glare, but she remained oblivious to him as she donned an odd-looking headset. Looking up, she said, "It's a Glenatat interface. I use it to speak directly to him, but I can bring our conversation up on my console for you to follow along."

She manipulated the controls. Hayden stood behind her and peered over her shoulder. She moved aside a little to give him access to the readout.

"According to the Glenatat's sentinel," he said, "that ship is phasing between normal and dark matter states."

"Is that even possible?" said Pavlovich.

"The Glenatat database says it is. The physics is beyond me, though—"

He gave Cora a questioning look.

"It looks like gibberish to me," she said.

Hayden regarded the image on the viewer that riveted the entire crew. "This is the location where we last encountered the Malliac."

"The one you said the girl killed?"

"Yes, sir."

"Get her in here."

A few tense minutes later, Stella entered the bridge. She gasped when she caught sight of the alien vessel on the display.

"I presume by your reaction that thing is familiar to you?" Pavlovich asked her.

She pressed her back to the bulkhead, as if attempting distance herself from it. "N...no. I've never seen that before."

The captain raised a skeptical eyebrow. "Are you sure?"

She stared at the image. "I... I didn't *see* it, but it feels...sort of the same, but almost as if it is only partly there. Does that make any sense?" She looked at Hayden. "How is it possible that we can see it?"

"We were hoping you could tell us," said Pavlovich. "Kaine thinks this is the ship you wrecked."

Beads of perspiration formed on her forehead as she turned back to the viewer. "I...I... don't know. It was all so fast."

Hayden spoke softly. "We think it's dead. I just hoped you could tell us something."

"Can you describe what took place?" asked the captain.

Stella nodded. She gently disengaged from Hayden's protective embrace and faced Pavlovich. "I can only try to explain the sensation. During the attack, it felt like I was connected to every one of them."

"You're sure they were the Malliac?"

"Oh, yes. I could not mistake that kind of experience for anything else."

"What happened?" asked Hayden.

"I... I was angry. I wanted to hurt them. I... reached out for them with my mind, and they suddenly went away. It was like a bunch of popping bubbles. Does that make any sense?"

He regarded the flickering vessel on the screen. "In a way, it does."

Pavlovich grumbled something inaudible to himself, then addressed Cora. "Is that wreck in any state for us to board it?"

"What are you thinking, Captain?" said Hayden.

"If we're to go up against them, now might be the ideal opportunity to study one of their ships for vulnerability or technology we can employ. I want to believe she could potentially think our enemies out of existence, but I don't want to rely on that ability. No offence implied, Miss Gabriel."

She shook her head. "None taken, Captain. I'm not sure how I did it or if I can do so again."

Pavlovich nodded, then turned back to Cora. "Well, Chief Engineer? Does your pet say we can board that thing?"

"He says it is physically there, but not temporally stable. Anyone who enters it will be ripped to shreds by the temporal tides."

"What the hell does that mean?"

"It... oh, it seemed so simple when he explained it."

"Take your time," said Hayden.

"That ship normally occupies multiple timelines simultaneously. But with its crew dead, parts of it begin leaking into something called null space."

"Is that why we can see it?"

"Yes, but then it drifts back into our dimension." Cora paused, listening to someone. "Alcon says that the Malliac and their ships can only function in our space-time when they are fully energized. He says that as time passes, they lose their ability to coexist with normal matter."

Pavlovich shifted in his seat. "Well, if we can't learn anything by boarding it, maybe it can tell us other things. Gunney, didn't you say you wanted something to shoot at?"

"Aye, Cap'n."

"It's time for a bit of target practice with the new weaponry. Let's see how it performs on that wreck."

"Yes, sir," said the cyborg, showing the most enthusiasm Hayden had ever seen from him. He thought he caught the hint of a smile flash across Gunney's ugly face.

"Cannon is locked."

"Fire at will."

Moments later, the lights dimmed as *Scimitar* spat a crimson bolt of energy at the derelict vessel. It struck one of the sections that was transitioning between states. It appeared to plunge into a deep stack of distorting mirrors. As the dark energy bored into it, the ship dissolved into a million glimmering pieces before it winked out of existence.

"Effective," said Pavlovich.

Hayden analyzed the results at his science station. He looked up. "How precisely can you target the cannon, Gunney?"

"At this range? To within a metre."

He returned to the terminal. "I'm sending you new coordinates. Please see if you can hit the location, if you don't mind."

The cyborg looked to Pavlovich. "Cap'n?"

A grin broke out on Pavlovich's face. "Do as he asks. I'm curious to learn what Kaine is up to."

Hayden looked up from the station. "The first bolt struck a part that was in transition. I want to see what it can do against a piece that is still stable."

"Targeting locked, sir."

"Let 'er rip," said the captain.

The dark energy pulse bored into its target. The spot seemed to collapse upon itself, distorting and dragging the vessel into a hole in space. Seconds later, the distorted region expanded in a brilliant blue light, and the derelict was ripped apart in an explosive chain reaction.

"Well, that was impressive."

"Now all we have to do is use that weapon to get close enough to the jump-control module," said Hayden.

"And hope it will be enough for us to fight our way out again," said Pavlovich. "Because those aliens will be pissed at us when we destroy that gate."

Taking the Fight to the Malliac

WITH NO REASON FOR further delay, the *Scimitar* departed for the Mu Arae jump-gate at one-half light speed.

"Miss Gabriel, you should remain on the bridge from this point onward. You're our canary."

"Sir?"

"It's a historical reference," said Hayden.

"Canaries were used in coal mines as a warning for gas build-up," said Pavlovich with a smile. "I don't fully trust the Glenatat technology."

"Of course," said Stella. She assumed a seat at an unoccupied bridge station. "But please remember that they can see me too."

Hayden was annoyed the captain chose that analogy. He had neglected to mention that the canary died.

"Is there a problem, Mister Kaine?"

"No, sir."

Pavlovich grunted and turned his attention elsewhere.

Hayden, noticing Stella's discomfort, approached her, and spoke quietly. "Are you all right?"

"There are a lot of strong emotions. I'm worried they will mask the Malliac from me."

"We can't really sedate the crew."

She smiled at his joke. "I just need to focus. I wish I could...attack them with my mind from here..."

"It'll be okay."

He squeezed her hand and returned to his station.

"How's our canary?" asked Pavlovich.

"She'll be fine, sir." Hayden spoke stiffly.

"Look, Kaine, I can either put her to use for me on the bridge or sedate her, so the enemy doesn't sniff her out and come looking for us. At this stage, we're going to encounter them anyway, so I see no point in knocking her out."

He clenched his jaw. "Yes, sir."

"I don't require your approval for either option regarding the girl, XO."

He scowled at Pavlovich, searching for words of outrage that would not form on his tongue.

"Captain!" Stella called out.

They both turned to see her doubled over in her chair, hands clutching her stomach. She looked up at them, her face pale and eyes filled with fear.

"I feel them. They're coming."

Hayden fought every instinct to rush to her aid but instead hurried to the science station.

Pavlovich's voice cut through the chatter on the bridge. "Everyone look alive. Kaine, is there anything on those new sensors?"

"Nothing so far—wait. Yes, two enemy ships approaching on intercept vectors. Passing coordinates to gunnery officer."

"I've got 'em," said Gunney. His raspy voice was charged with excitement.

"Well, score one for our little bird. She spotted them first." Pavlovich winked at Stella then ordered, "Give me a tactical display."

A schematic came up showing the positions of the *Scimitar* and the inbound Malliac vessels.

"It looks like they're both coming from the general direction of the jump-gate," said Hayden.

"They must perceive us as a threat, or else they wouldn't bother sending those ships at us."

"They might be reacting to Stella's presence."

Pavlovich grinned. "Let's give them a surprise party. Helm, accelerate to maximum sublight speed and point us at the nearest one of those bastards."

"Aye, sir," said Kwok after only a second of hesitation.

"Gunney, I'm giving you as much forward momentum as possible. Make our guns sing."

"Closest target is in my sights, Captain."

"Fire when ready."

Hayden's eyes were fixed on the display as the distance between *Scimitar* and the approaching vessel closed. The floor vibrated under the first volley.

He activated the controls and put up both the tactical and a forward view. The new imaging technology clearly showed the ship accelerating toward them.

He imagined the Glenatat-enhanced projectiles from the rail gun impacting whatever armour the Malliac possessed. He hoped their mass, increased by relativistic velocity, would rip through it like a bullet through paper.

The star-studded skies on the screen lit up as if a small sun went nova. In an instant, the other ship was gone.

A cheer erupted from the crew. Hayden noted relief on Pavlovich's face that mirrored his own. Their invisible foe could be beaten, and their mission had a real fighting chance of success.

Scimitar was rocked by an impact. Several people were knocked from their feet as the lights flickered and dimmed. The main viewer went dark, as did many of the workstations.

"A direct hit to our bow," shouted Cora above the chaos.

"Damage report," called Hayden as he scrambled to the science station.

"It looks like the enhanced armour took the brunt of the blast. An energy pulse put two of our engines offline. We are running on emergency auxiliary power."

"Get down there and get the everything turned back on," said Pavlovich. "We're blind and hurtling near light speed out of control. I don't like it."

She ran out the hatch.

"Kaine, can you see anything on instruments?"

"One Malliac ship is a million kilometres behind us, in pursuit and closing. It is twice the size of the one we took out. They hit us as we passed them."

"They're catching us? Helm, what is our present speed?"

"We got up to 0.79C before the engines went out."

"Estimated time until we are in their weapons range?" asked Pavlovich.

The bridge shook again.

"Never mind, I think I have my answer."

Hayden was at Cora's engineering console. "A hit to our stern section. The armour appears to be holding. I don't know how many more hits we can take until have a hull breach."

"Weapons status?"

"Aft rail guns are all out. There is power to the forward ones, but at the present relative velocity between our vessels, I don't know if they can pierce their armour."

"What about those dark energy cannons?"

"They're powered by the engines. With only two operational, I don't know if we can fire them."

"Damn it," said Pavlovich as he hit a comm switch on his chair. "Speak to me, Cora."

The bridge shook again from another Malliac barrage. A few seconds later, Cora's stressed voice came over the speaker.

"Working on it, Cap'n."

"Work faster. Is there enough juice to fire the cannons?"

"Just a sec, I need to ask Alcon."

Pavlovich scowled at his first officer and drummed his fingers.

"He says they'll operate on one engine, but the output won't be optimal."

The ship shook more violently as the Malliac closed the gap between the ships.

"Armour integrity is at risk," said Hayden. "The interval between their shots is consistent, Captain. They must need the time to recharge their weapons. If they're running their engines hot to catch us, it's possible they can't fire a full charge either."

Stella shivered. Pavlovich turned to her and said, "Can you do your wipe-out-all-the-bad-guys trick?"

"I... I don't know. I don't think so. I'm sorry."

"Hmph. Gunney, are the aft guns charged?"

"Yes, Cap'n."

"Then, please kick 'em in the balls."

The lights dimmed as *Scimitar* unleashed a volley from the energy cannon.

Hayden monitored the science station. "Direct hits. I think we damaged them."

The ship reeled under another barrage. He gripped the console to prevent being knocked from his chair.

"Hurt 'em again," said Pavlovich.

Once more they fired.

Hayden, eyes glued to the sensor readouts, called out, "I'm detecting micro fissures in their hull; at least I think that's what they are. They are flickering like we saw that other ship do. Gunney, I'm feeding you the coordinates. Try to concentrate your fire on those areas."

The cyborg nodded curtly. They were plunged into near darkness as the humming cannon drew the maximum available power.

The released energy erupted along the length of the cracks in the Malliac hull. Seconds later, the ship expanded into a brilliant blue flare before vanishing from the sensors.

"They are destroyed," said Kaine. "Completely obliterated."

"Cora, where are my engines?"

Pavlovich's inquiry seemed to jerk everyone's attention back to the moment, and they scrambled to prepare for the damage report request they all knew was coming.

"Five more minutes, Cap'n."

Pavlovich looked up from the comm panel and surveyed the crew. "Well done, people. Mister Kaine, we now know that we can dish it out better than they can. We may actually succeed at this crazy mission."

A Last Desperate Plan

"ENGINES ARE BACK ONLINE, Cap'n."

"Bloody well about time. Get your ass back to the bridge, Cora." Turning to the helmsman, he barked, "Kwok, get us to that jump-gate yesterday."

"Aye, Captain," answered the ensign as her hands were already inputting the commands.

Pavlovich turned to his XO. "How long until we arrive?"

Hayden hesitated over the readout screen.

"I'm waiting, First Officer."

"Um, sorry sir. We'll be there in two hours and sixteen minutes, but we've got a problem. A class six singularity is forming two million kilometres away from it."

Pavlovich pushed himself out of the chair. "How is that possible? The stolen singularities?"

"I believe so. Graviton spin decay signature is consistent with UEF engine specs. I'm also detecting multiple Malliac ships amassing near it."

"How many?"

"I'm still not used to these Glenatat instruments; something like thirty, of varying size and configuration." He looked up from the console. "And one of them has docked with the jump-gate station."

"Shit! We're too late."

"For what, Cap'n?" asked Cora as she entered the bridge.

Pavlovich said to her, "Watch the shop for a moment. Kaine, walk with me."

He hesitated until Pavlovich's scowl told him he was serious. As they walked down the corridor, the captain remained tight-lipped, and Hayden dared not inquire what was going on.

They ended up in front of the captain's quarters. The big man opened the door and gestured for him enter first.

Inside, with the door closed, Pavlovich indicated the empty chair while he went to the cabinet and removed a bottle. "Do you like Kentucky bourbon, Kaine?"

"Sir?"

He held up the bottle.

"Um, yes, please."

The captain poured them each a generous amount. After lifting their glasses in a silent toast, Pavlovich downed the contents in a single gulp.

Hayden took a tentative sniff of his before mimicking the older man. He struggled to match Pavlovich's gaze.

The captain broke out in laughter. "You're not a bourbon drinker, are you, Kaine?"

"No sir, more of a whisky sipper," he gasped.

"But you shot the drink anyway. Why?"

"Well, I suppose I didn't want to be rude."

"Bullshit. You thought it was a test, and you didn't want to lose face."

Hayden was unsure if the warmth he felt crawling up his face was the alcohol or his embarrassment. He nodded.

"Well, it isn't. I just needed a drink before we spoke."

"What is it you wanted to discuss, Captain?"

"I think you know. We're facing a no-win scenario."

"And you want my input."

"You're bloody right I want it, Kaine. I can only think of one solution, and it will cost every life on this ship. I need options."

Hayden studied the drops of liquor clinging to the inside of his glass. "I'm not sure there are many. The Malliac are poised to jump as soon as they hack the gate controls. We've got to destroy it if we're going to stop them."

"Which means we're going to have to fight our way past them. *Scimitar* is a good ship, with the best crew in the fleet, but we're outnumbered. Even with the new Glenatat hardware, we had a difficult time holding off two ships, but thirty of them..."

Hayden stared at the floor. "Possibly, with Stella's help, we can push our way through the armada, but..."

"I view your girlfriend as an unreliable weapon of last resort. Don't get me wrong, if I get the opportunity, I will use her, if she can make herself do it. I just want to ensure our effort will be worth it."

Silence hung over the room as both men contemplated the dilemma.

"Perhaps there is a way," said Hayden.

Pavlovich looked up; a smile barely hidden behind his beard. "Go on, First Officer."

"If the Malliac were distracted, a small craft could possibly slip past them and dock with the station."

"Now you're thinking like a military man. Go on."

"There is still the matter of the docked ship, but if I take a squad of Rangers with me..."

"You? You don't have the technical chops."

Hayden nodded. "I went over the specs with Cora. We only have to plant a singularity from one of our jump core chambers. The entire station will collapse into it, and the network will be destroyed. If I take Atan and some of her top shooters, we might be able to fight our way to inside."

"The odds..."

"Are too ridiculous to take seriously. This is a Hail Mary pass, Captain. Destroying the jump-gate with the rail gun or the dark energy cannon won't cut it. Transdimensional space will still be accessible to the Malliac if the station's core remains intact. All they need do is recover it, and everything is over for us."

"It's a suicide mission, Kaine."

"Sir, did you really believe any of us were getting out of this alive?"

"You would be wasted in the diplomatic corps, Lieutenant."

Hayden smiled. "I guess we'll never know."

"Well, since I can't think of any other option, we'll go with your plan. *Scimitar* will park between those ships and the black hole. With our light drive offline, there will be more power to devote to the energy cannons. Hopefully, we can hold them off long enough for you to complete your mission."

Hayden wondered how his father would react if he knew what he planned. Would he be proud of him, or disappointed by the mess he'd gotten himself into?

"Mister Kaine."

"Sir?"

"You have turned out to be an exemplary officer. My only regret is that I won't be able rub the admiral's nose in that fact."

It Is Done

STELLA'S SHIP WAS NOT small. In fact, it was roomy enough that she and her father had made a comfortable home of it for several years. Yet the squad of Rangers in their combat armour made it seem cramped. As Hayden manoeuvred the vessel toward the remaining docking port of the control station, he was glad for the short trip from *Scimitar*. He was more grateful they had not been detected.

Stella was to be thanked for that blessing. Despite Hayden's anticipation that she would insist on accompanying him, she had volunteered to remain behind.

"If I stay on the ship, I can distract their attention from you. You'll never make it past them otherwise."

Not for the first time, she astounded him with her altruism. Though she was raised isolated from human society, her commitment to the greater good made him feel a deep sense of shame for what drove his life choices.

She and Pavlovich had conspired behind his back, leaving him little choice but to accept their plan. *Scimitar* would park itself between the enemy fleet and the black hole. Stella agreed to be the bait to draw the enemy's attention.

It was difficult to leave her behind. He realized how irrational that regret was; everyone would likely be dead within an hour. Still, until his departure, he had entertained the romantic notion that the two of them might die in each other's arms. Instead, they only managed to steal a few minutes alone before duty called them both. After an all-too-short embrace and a final kiss, he was aboard the small vessel with a group of grim, silent Rangers.

He piloted the ship to the station's second docking bay without seeming to attract any attention.

"We have a positive seal."

Warrant Officer Atan nodded and donned her helmet. In her full combat gear, she and the six other soldiers resembled armoured giants as they faced the hatch, preparing themselves for what lay on the other side.

Hayden had opted to wear light body armour so he could retain maximum mobility. His job was not to engage Malliac warriors; the Rangers were for that. His sole purpose was to plant the device that rested beside him.

A tuned singularity extracted from one of *Scimitar*'s light drive engines resided inside a containment unit. The cylindrical package, about the size of his forearm, was to be planted as close as possible to the central reactor. On detonation, the confinement field would be collapsed, and the singularity would consume everything in its proximity.

According to Cora, once the reaction core was consumed, the connecting filaments that connected their universe to transdimensional space would be destroyed. The black hole created by the Malliac would no longer be an entry point for them into the network.

Of course, to be effective, he had to get to the reactor. The likelihood of that depended on how far they could penetrate the station before they were detected.

Their modified dark energy weapons at the ready, the Rangers exited the craft in a staggered, defensive formation until only he remained aboard. Several seconds later, he received the all-clear signal.

Ignoring the butterflies in his stomach, he followed the soldiers.

The place seemed abandoned.

He checked his helmet controls to ensure the Glenatat modifications were turned on. On confirming there were no Malliac in the vicinity, he forced himself to breathe.

After displaying the route on his HUD, he nodded to Atan to proceed as planned.

The Rangers pressed around him, Atan and three in front and the balance protecting their backs. In single file, they inched down the corridor. The advance guard checked and cleared every doorway and intersecting passage.

Though the facility was smaller than *Scimitar*, it was still far larger than he had appreciated. It took the squad a few minutes to reach the sealed entrance to the chamber.

He entered the universal override codes given him by Pavlovich. He hoped they were current as he input the final digit.

The door opened to two Malliac soldiers. Almost three metres tall, they were encased in obsidian battle armour that seemed to glow from within. Multiple, insectoid arms with pincers held deadly appearing weapons.

He cried out and stumbled back. Even as he fumbled to unholster his own blaster, one of the creatures fired at the hapless Ranger he had fallen into.

Chaos unfolded with an exchange of weapons fire. His modified small firearm had no effect on the shielded alien, which turned its weapon upon him.

A high-energy arm cannon took the Malliac out. It hurtled into its companion, knocking them both to the floor. Atan advanced into the open doorway to unleash a second fatal blast.

As he struggled back to his feet, movement farther down the corridor caught his attention.

"More of them are coming!"

Knowing full well his gun was ineffectual, he directed fire at the alien that rounded the corner. Two Rangers joined him in targeting the creature, which collapsed under their withering barrage.

Something seized him by the shoulder and yanked him inside the chamber. He turned to see it was Atan's iron grip that had pulled him out of the firefight.

Anticipating his question, she said, "Sorry, sir, but you're no match for them, and you're the only one who can get to the core with the bomb."

Hayden looked to the doorway to see that three of the squad were down. The surviving Rangers entered and sealed the door.

"It won't be long before they break through. We'll cover you for as long as we can, sir."

The sick realization sank in that none of them would leave the station. If their lives were to mean anything, he had to ensure the package he came to plant did its job.

Stepping over dead Malliac, he advanced to the chamber door. After a last look at Atan and the others, he opened it and entered.

Though he had once toured a jump-gate control station during his time at the academy, that one was under construction and not active. The sight that greeted him overwhelmed his senses. The walls glowed, bathed in a brilliant, shifting spectrum of colours. Hayden was forced to override the filter of his visor so that he could make out details.

In the middle of the cylindrical chamber, set like an axis, was the reaction core. It extended to the ceiling. Looking down, he noticed he stood on a transparent floor and saw the pillar continue down below him. The column pulsed with a blue light while the room thrummed in time with it. The room seemed to beat like a giant heart.

As he secured the singularity bomb, he realized that the cardiac analogy was not inappropriate. In a few moments he would cut off the beating pulse of human civilization, setting his species back by half a millennium, perhaps even dooming it to extinction.

Out of a sense of hope, Cora had built in a delay timer to give him time to get away. He turned it on and sat on the floor with his back to the console.

Unholstering his firearm, he cradled it in his lap and laughed. He hoped that the Rangers could hold off the aliens until the bomb went off. If he was supposed to be final line of defence, his modified pop gun would not be of much use.

He suppressed the urge to contact his escort. The last thing they needed was to be pestered about how the battle was going.

Heavy blows against the reaction chamber door told him the whole story. Atan and the others were dead, and he would soon join them. He was worried that the door might not withstand whatever they had to use against it for the time he had left.

Standing, he checked the readout. Several minutes remained. Cora had been generous when she provided for his escape. He searched the simple interface for an override button but failed to locate one. Sighing, he pointed his weapon at it.

The purpose of the bomb was to rupture the suspension field that kept the singularity from interacting with anything. All he needed to do was destroy the container, and he and everything around him would be instantly sucked into the oblivion of a micro black hole. The network would be destroyed and his mission accomplished.

A simple pull of the trigger, and the mission would be accomplished.

Visions of Stella prevented him from doing it.

He tried to imagine what was happening to her and the others aboard *Scimitar*. Even heavily armoured and with the enhanced firepower provided by the Glenatat, he had a difficult time imagining that they could withstand the onslaught of the Malliac fleet for long.

If he didn't act, the enemy would soon breach the doorway. He and everyone he ever knew or cared for would be dead by their hands. Human history would be wiped away, along with every other sentient species in the galaxy.

How could a race be so malevolent? What drove them? Was it instinct? Were compassion and reason beyond them? He chuckled at the idea that he might be able to talk to them, negotiate with them to find another path.

A heavy blow at the door yanked him from those fanciful thoughts. He inhaled deeply and steadied his shaking hand as he resolved to fire his gun the moment the door failed.

Nothing happened.

The incessant beating on the heavily armoured door had stopped.

Hayden waited, anxiously anticipating a renewed assault. Perhaps they were preparing to use explosives. He looked at the remaining time on the bomb, considering the option of not waiting and guaranteeing the fulfillment of his mission.

Had they somehow anticipated what he was up to and abandoned the station?

A burst of static sounded in his helmet receiver, and he thought he heard Atan's voice. Had she stopped the Malliac attackers after all? Perhaps she was injured.

"Atan? Is that you? Status report! Chief?"

"Bzzt...zzzpt...nemy dow...all clear—bzzt."

He took a final look at the countdown clock and made some computations. There was still time to escape. Atan and maybe others needed his help.

He made up his mind.

Advancing to the door, he cautiously opened it.

A horrific scene greeted him. He was reminded of a museum painting his father once showed him titled "The Gates of Hell."

Near the doorway, he stepped over the remains of two Malliac soldiers. Farther away lay others, some with their armour ripped apart. Scattered among them were the armoured husks of the human Rangers. They had put up a superhuman resistance, overcoming twice their number.

He searched for Atan or anyone who might still live. Spotting a Ranger beneath an alien body, he recognized Atan's warrant officer insignia. Rushing to her side, he called out to her as he pushed aside a blaster, still attached to an arm.

He removed her helmet and gasped at the sight of her lifeless face.

A quick search of the other human bodies confirmed that none of the Rangers had survived. He glanced back at the two creatures lying by the door. Neither had signs of weapons damage, and he briefly wondered how that was possible before remembering the countdown timer.

He picked up one of the lighter guns from a fallen Ranger and entered the corridor. A furtive glance up and down revealed it to be abandoned.

He bolted from the room, desperate to reach his docked ship. Giving little thought to what he might do if he encountered any more of the aliens, he arrived at the airlock without incident.

Less than a minute later, his vessel fired engines at full burn to put as much distance as possible between him and the station.

Suddenly, in his wake, the blackness of space was illuminated by a brilliant flare of the exploding bomb. The expanding fireball reached its maximum radius before it pulsed, as if violently reaching the end of a leash. Just as quickly, the sphere of heat and light collapsed on itself, extinguished like a candle.

It was done. Any sign of the station or the alien ship that was docked to it was gone, along with any means of return to Earth. The Malliac were stopped and no longer a threat to the rest of the galaxy. Instead of being proud, he couldn't help but think he'd made a terrible mistake.

He checked his navigation console. Reconciling his position, he searched for *Scimitar*, worried nothing remained of it.

Shortly, he found it and brought an image up on the screen.

What he saw was impossible.

Gone

THE BATTLE WAS MIRACULOUSLY over, and *Scimitar* had carried the day, as unimaginable as that was. Dozens of Malliac ships were adrift. Many of them flickered, just like the wreck they'd encountered by the wormhole.

Nearer the black hole drifted the severely wounded ship. A significant part of her bow was gone, and fires burned in the aft engineering section.

Hayden's heart pounded as he adjusted course to rendezvous with the vessel. His spirits sank further with every unsuccessful attempt to raise her on the comm.

As he approached, he noted the ship's hangar was destroyed, so he located an intact docking port and manoeuvred his ship toward it.

The seal was marginal, another miracle considering the beating *Scimitar* had taken. He forced the inner doors open and peered into the lightless interior.

Playing his torchlight along the corridor, he did not recognize what he saw. Detritus and bodies floated, as if suspended in water. The walls were scorched, and blown panels revealed damaged conduit casing.

Though *Scimitar* was obviously without gravity or power, the positive docking seal told him this section still had atmospheric pressure. He decided to keep his helmet on for the light and to filter out any toxins from the fires.

His pulse pounded in his ears as he pulled himself along, past body after body of people he had spoken with only hours before.

Not sure where to search, he made his way to the bridge. It was the most protected section, and he hoped he would find survivors there, including Stella.

Fires and debris blocked his route, forcing him to find an alternate one. With every metre he advanced, his hope that anyone was alive diminished. The ship appeared to be crewed only by the dead.

Finally reaching his goal, he found the hatch barely hanging from its hinges. Using a piece of debris, he levered the door open enough for him to enter. His heart sank at what he saw.

The bridge had fared little better than the rest of *Scimitar*. Small fires burned, obscuring his view.

He called out, hoping someone was alive to hear him.

Someone coughed in the gloom. His pulse raced as he followed the sound to the place where Stella normally sat. He gasped at the sight of her. Still strapped in, her arms floated, slack, in front of her. Her eyes were closed, and he feared the worst. On reaching her, he saw her chest rise and fall. She coughed as he unbuckled her harness and enfolded her in his arms.

Playing his light around, he saw nobody else. Twice more he shouted into the darkness, hoping someone would answer, but silence was his only reward.

Holding Stella, he pulled his way back through the hatchway to return to his docked vessel.

As he passed the passage leading to the engineering section, he thought he heard voices shouting. He called out repeatedly, but nobody responded.

Realizing Stella needed oxygen, he decided to get her to his ship before he returned to search for more survivors.

Once aboard, he settled her into a seat and applied the emergency O2 mask. Her ragged breathing eased. Despite his gentle effort to rouse her, she would not respond. Inspecting her for injuries, he found none, not even a mark on her head that would explain her unconsciousness.

Hayden was a loss as to what to do for her.

As he considered leaving her to go search for other survivors, an alarm sounded on the pilot's console. The confusing readout showed elevated neutrino and graviton particle densities.

Only when the ship lurched, and metal screeched in complaint did he realize what was happening. They were being pulled into the gravity well of the black hole.

Settling into the pilot seat, he thought he might be able to stabilize their position with his ship's engines. The computer, however, quickly persuaded him of the futility of his plan. The power necessary to pull them back out to a safe distance was beyond his small vessel's rating.

With no real choice available, he released the docking clamps and fired his main thrusters at full burn. He prayed he wasn't too late to escape the same fate as *Scimitar*.

The overtaxed engines screamed. The tiny vessel fought to overcome the deadly grip of gravity. Perspiration dripped from Hayden's brow as the temperature in the cabin rose. The whine of the straining power plant was deafening.

Little by little, his ship increased the distance between the vessels. His engines complained loudly, and he was worried the stresses would rip the vessel apart.

Finally, the emergency alarm stopped, indicating he had escaped danger. He shut down everything to let it all cool and checked the rearview screen.

Inexorably, *Scimitar* fell toward the event horizon. Within a few seconds it would pass into a place from which even light couldn't escape. If anyone remained alive, they wouldn't realize what happened to them as time slowed to a crawl under the tremendous gravitational distortion of space and time.

With a sudden brilliant blue-green flash, *Scimitar* vanished. Hayden had never witnessed anything plunge into a black hole before. Perhaps the flare was a response of the ship's jump engine core as it crossed the event horizon.

He wiped a tear from his cheek as he took a moment to remember the gallant crew of the *Scimitar*. No monuments would ever be built for them, because the story of their sacrifice would never be heard. Only Hayden knew, but now, trapped across the galaxy, he couldn't tell anyone.

Explanations

A COUGH FROM THE REAR of the ship roused him from his musing, and he hurried to Stella's side. She struggled to remove the oxygen mask. Her eyelids fluttered as she fought to awaken.

"Easy there," said Hayden as he replaced the breathing apparatus. "Let's keep that on for a few more minutes."

She calmed at the sound of his voice and relaxed back into the pillow. Slowly, she forced her eyes open and tried to focus on him. With a joyful gasp, she wrapped her arms about his neck, burying her face in his shoulder.

After a long moment, he gently broke the embrace to look at her tear-streaked face.

"Where are we?" Her voice was muffled by the mask.

"We're on your ship," he said.

"The others?"

He shook his head. "I didn't find anyone else alive."

"I thought I would never see you again." Her tears began anew.

"I thought the same," he said, going on to explain how he found her. "What happened aboard *Scimitar*?"

She removed the respirator and closed her eyes. Wiping the wetness from her cheeks, she sat up and looked into Hayden's eyes. "The battle was not going well. Captain Pavlovich and Gunney managed to damage or destroy a number of their ships, but there were too many of them...I'm sorry, so much happened...it all blurs together..."

"Take your time." He tried to reassure her with his smile.

"What I vividly remember is, one moment the captain was cursing, and the next the bridge was filled with shouting, flames, and smoke. Hayden, it was horrifying! All I could sense, see, or hear was chaos. Everyone's panic seemed to crash down on top of me. And there was the other presence that rose above it all."

"The Malliac."

She nodded. "They hung over everything. The malice—the pure hatred—it tightened about me. I thought it would overwhelm me."

Tears flowed down her cheeks. "It was the crew who saved me. I clung to every dying echo of human emotion from them. They were my only anchor. No matter how terrifying, sharing their experiences was infinitely more bearable than facing the Malliac."

"I don't understand—"

"They enveloped me like a toxic cloud, until they were the only thing that seemed to exist. Imagine being smothered by something so totally alien that there is no human experience to describe it. I couldn't tell if I still breathed or if my heart was beating. All I knew was that they fed off me; feasted on all the fear and terror from every crew member that flowed into me. I sensed more and more of them join in their violation of me in a perverse feeding frenzy."

Hayden wrapped his arms around her. She sobbed into his shoulder and her words poured forth. "I was an exposed nerve. The slightest emotion from anyone around me who was still alive stung like a thousand whips. I couldn't do anything to make it stop; I tried to recall a happy memory—something that might anchor me to my humanity. I fought to remember Papa's stories about my mother."

Her eyes were wide as she relived her violation. "It wasn't fear or terror or anger or agony they wanted. Hayden, I was so wrong!"

She clung to him and shivered as she agonizingly relived her experience.

"It was *me*. I was like an addictive drug to them, and they couldn't get enough. They would drain me of my experiences and abilities until nothing remained, and still hunger for more.

"I knew in that moment that if they ever gained access to the greater part of humanity, there would be no stopping them. They had learned what was possible because of their connection to me. Next time, I knew they wouldn't need an empath to satisfy their addiction. Every living person would become prey, and humankind would be hunted into extinction, ripped apart from the inside, with no defence."

Her breathing slowed, and with it her shaking. She looked up at him with an unfamiliar, frightening expression. Inconsolable grief and guilt battled with a triumph and satisfaction. Gazing at her, he realized what had happened to the Malliac.

"You told them, 'no' again," he said softly.

Her eyes widened in recollection. She shook her head sadly. "It wasn't like the last time. That time I wanted to protect you more than anything else. Then all I could think of then was my love for you. I thought it was the strength of that emotion that countered and overcame my fear and destroyed them. I was so wrong."

"Then what was it?"

She broke from his embrace and moved away from Hayden, as if repelled by his touch.

"Everyone around me was dead. I was alone. Pavlovich thought you failed your mission, and I allowed myself to be convinced there was no way you survived. I believed him because I couldn't sense you."

"Stella, that is an easy enough thing to believe, given the distance—"

"You don't understand. I can always feel you. Even when you docked with the station and went inside, I felt your fear; your anger and regret."

"Then, wha—?"

"When the Malliac overwhelmed me, I lost that connection. It was easy to succumb to the notion you had died, and I despaired. The only thing I wanted was to strike back in revenge, and that is what I did. I gave them access to everything. I held nothing of me back, including my will for them to pay for taking your life."

Silence fell between them. He tried to digest the magnitude of what she had said.

"It's my fault," she said between sobs.

"You can't take responsibility for what those aliens wanted."

"Yes, I can. I must accept the truth."

"You're not making sense."

"I lied to you. I've been able to control my power since I was a little girl. How do you think we survived all these years?"

"Why didn't you tell me?"

"I was afraid of losing you if you found out about me."

He thought she exaggerated, still emotionally drained from her experience. "What are you talking about?"

"We didn't spend our lives cowering from the Malliac," she said. "Once Father learned what I could do, he turned the tables on them. We began to hunt them, using the singularities we recovered as bait to draw them in. Then it was my job to destroy them. It was so easy. It was like simply being near me was fatal to them."

"I..." Hayden searched for words.

She said, "You don't know what it's like to touch them. In the early days, they had no first-hand experience with humans. When they encountered me, an empath, a door opened for them that they couldn't resist entering. I was a highly addictive drug for them, and it was easy for me to give them a fatal dose of what they craved."

"What changed?"

"They grew more resistant. What once satisfied them was no longer enough, and I had to allow them to access deeper emotions and experiences to achieve the same effect. After each incident, I required more time to recover and to regain my familiarity with my humanity. I changed, and as time progressed, through every encounter, those Malliac who didn't die gained some of my knowledge.

"Through me they came to understand my father's research to break into the jump-gate station. Eventually, Papa realized the danger I was. He broke off the hunt, and we went into hiding. He kept me sedated so they couldn't find me, but the damage was already done. They had everything they needed to hack the jump-gate."

"Why didn't you tell me?"

"Father wanted it to remain a secret, and after I got to know you, I was too ashamed to mention it. I didn't think they were able to use the information they took from me."

"It was you who tipped off the Glenatat?"

She nodded. "They learned about it when they first scanned me. They analyzed the data and determined that the Malliac were capable of accessing jump space."

He wandered back to the pilot's station. The monitor still displayed the dead armada.

Stella joined him and stood just out of arm's reach. She looked at him with heartbreak in her eyes, began to speak but stifled herself.

He turned and embraced her. Pulling her close, he kissed the top of her head. They stared at where *Scimitar* had once been. Part of him hoped if he waited long enough, the ship would pop back into existence.

"We stopped them. There was an enormous price for that victory, but at least humanity can go on to rebuild."

"But it cost you everything."

He smiled, marvelling at his reaction to her words. "It just doesn't seem all that important anymore."

He didn't know how many of the aggressive alien race still existed, but they were still a threat. Thankfully, they, like everyone else now, was relegated to slower-than-light travel. With luck, the messengers the Glenatat had returned home got the word out to enough of the colony worlds about the danger. It would be more than a decade before the

Malliac expansion reached the nearest human populated planet. Perhaps, forewarned, humanity would be able to defend itself from the inevitable arrival.

As far as he was concerned, his part in the fight was over. His life was now predetermined in an entirely different way. Now he was marooned in an inaccessible star system, with no chance of ever getting back to his old life. He'd gotten his wish and broken free of his father's control.

He hugged her tightly. What he gained was nothing he ever expected possible. He hoped he deserved this new life.

A New Dawn

HAYDEN OPENED THE BLINDS and blinked at the bright dawn.

"Mmm, is it morning so soon?" Stella rolled over and covered her head with the covers.

Smiling, he returned to the bed and tickled her exposed neck with soft kisses.

"Time to get up, sleepy-head."

She threw the pillow playfully at him.

He embraced her, both laughing as they wrestled until they fell to the floor.

Lying in each other's arms, they basked in Mu Arae's warmth.

"What is Earth like?" she asked.

He paused, a smile on his lips. Not long ago, mention of his now lost home would have dredged up sadness and regret.

"It is a beautiful world—but crowded. Not like here."

They and a small group of survivors of the Malliac scourge had settled on Ricote, the largest moon orbiting the fourth planet in the system. It was the only body with a breathable atmosphere and near Earth-normal gravity.

"Do you miss it?"

He looked down on her sleepy face and considered the question. "Sometimes." There was no point in lying to her. "I occasionally wonder about my life that might have been."

"And?"

He sighed. "I realize how shallow my existence was."

"So, you're telling me that you are happier being a salvager here with me than you would be ruling an empire?"

He leaned over and kissed her. "I can't think of any place I would rather find myself."

She hugged him then got up to go to the toilet.

Hayden rose and made them both some tea.

Steaming cup in hand, he sat down at the terminal. It was his morning ritual to review the sensor record of *Scimitar*'s final moments. He was determined their sacrifice would never be forgotten, and he made it his mission to purposefully remember every crew member on a regular basis.

Someday their story would be known to the outside world. Whenever a long-distance courier drone was dispatched from Ricote, he ensured that an account of the events was included. It would be decades before anyone read them, but it was all he could do.

Something caught his eye that he hadn't noticed before. He reran playback to convince himself he hadn't imagined it.

Slowing the record, he studied every image until the anomaly appeared. Freezing the vid, he examined it using some of the other EM bands.

"What are you doing, Hayden?"

"Stella," he said excitedly, "look at this."

He played the enhanced recording for her.

"There. Did you see that? Five milliseconds before *Scimitar* should have crossed the event horizon, there was a flash in the engine section, and she vanished."

"What could it mean?" she asked.

"I don't know, but they didn't drop into that black hole."

"Is it possible the ship survived? That someone was still alive?"

"I really don't know," said Hayden, "but it is a hopeful idea, isn't it?"

Free book offer

FREE EBOOK OFFER!

As a way of saying thank you for purchasing this novel, I want to offer you a free ebook.

To claim your free story please join my reader list by going to

https://www.prudenauthor.com/Kaine1-free-offer

About the Author

D.M.(DOUG) PRUDEN WORKED for 35 years in the petroleum industry as a geophysicist. For most of his life he has been plagued with stories banging around inside his head that demanded to be let out into the world. He currently spends his time as an empty nester in Calgary, Alberta, Canada with his long-suffering wife of many years. When he isn't writing science fiction stories, he likes to spend his time playing with his grandchildren and working on improving his golf handicap.

Don't miss out!

Visit the website below and you can sign up to receive emails whenever D.M. Pruden publishes a new book. There's no charge and no obligation.

https://books2read.com/r/B-A-MNWD-GALX

BOOKS 2 READ

Connecting independent readers to independent writers.

Did you love *Kaine's Sanction*? Then you should read *Kaine's Retribution*[1] by D.M. Pruden!

An empire has fallen, and civilization tears itself apart.

But there is a way to restore it all.

Ten years ago, the Malliac invasion was averted, but at the cost of humanity's interstellar transit network. Trapped at the edge of human-occupied space, Hayden Kaine languishes in guilt and regret over his role in dooming a thousand worlds to permanent isolation.

Then, after being lost for a decade, his old ship and crew mysteriously reappear, bringing with them an alien technology. Kaine seizes the opportunity to rejoin his companions in the hope they can repair the damage that has been done and restore the empire.

---

1. https://books2read.com/u/mdLRQW

2. https://books2read.com/u/mdLRQW

But Scimitar holds the key to an even more valuable secret, one which is coveted by many powerful men and places the lives of his companions in danger.

With time running out, Kaine must decide who he can trust, otherwise, not only will his friends be doomed, but the galaxy will be plunged into a civil war that will cost billions of lives.

Read more at www.prudenauthor.com.

Also by D.M. Pruden

Future Vistas
Future Vistas Vol 1

Mars Ascendant
The Ares Weapon
Mother of Mars
Child of Mars
Legacy of Mars
Mars Ascendant Box Set: Books 1-4

Requiem's Run
Armstrong Station
Phobos Station
Rhea's Vault
Ganymede Station
The Jovian Collective

Shattered Empire

Kaine's Sanction
Kaine's Retribution
Kaine's Reparation
Shattered Empire Omnibus: Books 1-3

Standalone
Throwing Stones

Watch for more at www.prudenauthor.com.